W9-BJR-748

GET IT RIGHT THE
FIRST TIME . . .

With a snarl, Lang turned on Torwald, his finger tightening on the trigger.

"Wait, Lang," Kiril said. "We need to talk."

"I'm listening."

"Look, this thing has gone sour." She staggered away from Michelle and walked up to Lang, her left forearm cradled in her right hand. "Look, Lang, give me a break. I'm gonna be close to Izquierda, Lang. I can make it worth your while to help me out."

The mercenary gleam came into Lang's eyes. "Yeah, what're you gonna give me, little girl?"

She was close enough now. "This." Before the word was finished, her knife had gone in below his jaw. She had never used one to kill before, but she knew how it was done. She got it right the first time.

SPACER:
WINDOW OF
THE MIND

JOHN MADDOX ROBERTS

ACE BOOKS, NEW YORK

This book is an Ace original edition,
and has never been previously published.

SPACER: WINDOW OF THE MIND

An Ace Book / published by arrangement with
the author

PRINTING HISTORY
Ace edition / April 1988

All rights reserved.
Copyright © 1988 by John Maddox Roberts.
Cover art by Richard Hescox.
This book may not be reproduced in whole or in part,
by mimeograph or any other means, without permission.
For information address: The Berkley Publishing Group,
200 Madison Avenue, New York, New York 10016.

ISBN: 0-441-77787-2

Ace Books are published by The Berkley Publishing Group,
200 Madison Avenue, New York, New York 10016.
The name ''ACE'' and the ''A'' logo
are trademarks belonging to Charter Communications, Inc.
PRINTED IN THE UNITED STATES OF AMERICA

10 9 8 7 6 5 4 3 2 1

This book is dedicated to General Winston Kratz: a pioneer pilot, who contributed enthusiasm, love, and ingenuity not only to the field of aviation, but to life. And to Anne Scarborough Kratz, a beloved aunt, with thanks and gratitude for their encouragement and assistance.

1

Kiril risked a glance over her left shoulder. The killers were still behind her. She scrambled on bare feet over the rubble of a half-collapsed building. There was a narrow alley to her right and she ducked into it. Maybe they wouldn't see the move and would pass up the alley. She had not been quick enough. "There she is!" a voice yelled. Without breaking stride, she stooped and snatched up a fist-sized chunk of plasticrete. On her next stride, she pivoted on the ball of one foot, spun and threw it, continuing the spin and continuing to run down the alley with almost no time lost. She heard a man yell with pain, and she grinned. It would make no difference. They were going to kill her pretty soon, but there was still some satisfaction in drawing blood.

As she ran, her mind unrolled a map of the area ahead of her. Nobody knew the slums of Civis Astra as well as Kiril. A life of constant danger spent amid the planless tangle of alleys and streets of the sprawling slum had honed her sense of direction and location to preternatural sharpness. She had grown up amid the festering tenements and ruinous structures of long-forgotten purpose, and she knew every cellar and every dank doorway. But, she reflected ruefully, her pursuers, collectively, knew the place just as well. And there were hundreds of them, or would be soon. By now, word of the reward was all over the city.

She chanced another look back and her blood chilled. Khan was among them. No doubt about it, she was doomed. Pao Lin only sent Khan out on the most serious missions, when there was a mark who absolutely had to be killed, with no chance of failure. Khan used a thump gun, so called from its muffled report. Its explosive charge propelled twenty or so soft-metal pellets in a spreading cloud. It was a primitive weapon, but devastating at short range in the narrow alleys of Civis Astra when used in the hands of an expert. And Khan was an expert. He wasn't just good at killing, he loved it.

She decided on the Gambler's Warren. She knew she was going to die anyway, but it was her nature to try to live as long as possible. It was this quality that had caused her to cling so tenaciously to a life many would not have considered to be worth living on any terms. As long as she had one breath, she was going to fight for the next.

The Gambler's Warren was an area of tiny booths and stalls, low dives and dope houses, smuggler's shops and receiving houses for stolen goods. It was the oldest part of the city, its streets and alleys an unplanned jumble dating from the planet's frontier days. It was a maze, its passages so twisted and bewildering that she just might lose them and earn another miserable, sleepless night. Such nights were the kind she was used to, and worth pursuing.

She still had a way to go before she reached the Warren. The city of Civis Astra, "City of the Stars," had been named, somewhat optimistically, by the first pioneers to settle on Thoth. That had been during the early days of humanity's expansion from Earth. It had been a heady, optimistic time. From a backwoods colony, Thoth had progressed to become a prosperous, self-supporting world. Then had come the long years of agonizing upheaval caused by the great series of interplanetary conflicts known, simply, as the War. With the War came an endless stream of refugees, pouring into Thoth as their planets were invaded, turning the cities into overpopulated slums. Civis Astra had become the most bloated slum of all. Eventually the War had ended, but many worlds were left incapable of supporting their former populations. It would be many years before economies recovered enough to open new worlds. In the meantime, the refugees stayed where they were, and a generation had grown up knowing nothing but squalor, hunger, and want.

She ducked down a side alley, jumped over a couple of fences, crossed a vacant lot, and was in the Warren. It was early evening and the place was not yet heavily populated. People who frequented the Warren were not, for the most part, the type to welcome the light of day. It couldn't have been better. Her judgment had been good, her instincts hadn't failed her. Unfortunately, her timing was all wrong. She had always known that you could avoid just about any kind of trouble or danger by using your wits, but there wasn't much you could do about plain bad luck.

She didn't see the big man until it was too late to stop. He stepped out of a fence's shack and straight into her path. She ran into him with such force that she bounced back and landed in the gutter. The man bent to help her up, but she was too stunned to rise. She could feel blood trickling from her nose as she looked up at him. Automatically, she sized him up as if he were a potential mark.

He was a tall man, dressed in a gray Earth spacer's coverall and Spacer Marine boots. He wore a vest of some kind of reptile hide that was iridescent blue-green. His hair was grizzled and his face deeply tanned. He didn't look like the kind she would try to brace, and for a dazed moment she wondered whether he might be another of Pao Lin's hatchetmen.

"You all right, kid?" he asked with some concern.

"Not hardly," she said. "Just let me go, spacer, I've got to get out of here." She tried to yell the words but they came out in a wheezing gasp. Her lungs still felt half paralyzed. She looked about desperately. It was too late. Khan was there. Khan was huge, as tall as the spacer and much wider. The thump gun looked like a toy in his immense hands. His flat face held no more expression than a wooden idol's.

"Stand aside, Earthie," Khan said. "She's mine."

"You mean she belongs to you? She's your property?" The

spacer's thumbs were now hitched in his belt. Kiril was still huddled at his feet. She felt almost able to stand, but there seemed to be little point. The thump gun had two barrels, and it would be one for the spacer, the other for her. She was still looking for a way out, though.

"I have orders to kill her," Khan said. "Orders from Pao Lin."

"I don't know Pao Lin," the spacer said. "And I don't like to see kids killed."

Khan shrugged and raised the thump gun. Kiril braced herself for the blast that would kill both of them. She wouldn't close her eyes in her last moment, but stared directly at Khan. Above her the spacer moved so quickly that his hand was a blur as it darted beneath his vest and emerged with a laser. He burned a hole neatly through Khan's shoulder before the killer could line up his thump gun. There was a spurt of smoke and flame from Khan's tunic and he dropped, his eyes already glazing with deep shock.

"Real nice, spacer," Kiril said. "But we're not out of it yet." She was still sure she was going to die. There were too many on her trail. If a hundred were not enough, there would be more. No K'ang leader like Pao Lin could let one marked for death escape, whatever the cost. Even if the original offense had been trivial, his face was at stake. Pao Lin was not about to lose face over one skinny girl. Four men appeared at the head of the alley. One spoke into a communicator as they spotted Khan's inert form. The spacer stepped past Kiril and picked up Khan's thump gun. He held it casually as the four approached.

"I don't know who you are, mister," said the one with the communicator, "but that cully's marked for the big one. You got Khan, but there's four of us." The speaker was a rangy man in a ragged green tunic. He held a slug pistol, and the others had knives and hatchets. The spacer looked with bemusement at the thump gun he held.

"I haven't seen one of these things in years," he said. "Used to be pretty good with one, though. Now, at this range, I'll bet I can chop the four of you down with one shot." He lined up the weapon with the same startling speed he had shown in drawing on Khan.

"Maybe you can," said the speaker. "But we're dead

anyway, if we don't finish that one.''

"There's a difference,'' said the spacer. ''It's maybe die later or certainly die now.'' They thought it over, then started backing away. When they reached the end of the alley, they turned and scattered in four directions. The spacer hauled Kiril to her feet and gave her a shove.

"Run,'' he ordered.

"Where?''

"Toward the spaceport. My ship's there.'' They began running. Kiril had her breath back now, and another adrenaline surge gave her renewed energy. As he ran, the spacer took out a belt communicator. He barked into it rapidly. ''*Space Angel! Space Angel!* This is Torwald. I'm headed for the ship. I've got a mob after me, real killers. Send K'Stin and B'Shant to meet me in front of the Spacer's Hall. Hurry up!''

"Tor, sometimes you're more trouble than you're worth,'' said a disembodied voice.

They ran until Kiril was almost ready to collapse from exhaustion. Almost, but not quite. Luckily, the Warren was adjacent to the spaceport, which hadn't changed location since the planet had first been settled. They emerged from a littered alleyway into a small square where the Spacer's Hall was located. A few spacers in search of employment were lounging on the steps, and they looked with interest at the two fugitives. Kiril saw twenty or thirty men erupting from other alleys and streets, pouring into the square. They were the reinforcements Pao Lin's men had called for. They must have intercepted the spacer's transmission.

"Sorry, spacer,'' Kiril said. ''Looks like your friends didn't make it. Remember, I didn't ask you to interfere.'' She scanned the mob of men who were closing in on them. They were ragged and looked hungry. None was a killer as efficient as Khan, but she knew there wasn't one among them who wouldn't kill his best friend to earn Pao Lin's goodwill.

"Get that pistol out and zap a few, spacer,'' Kiril said. ''We're gonna die anyway, it'd be a shame not to take a few with us.'' A pair of thin-bladed daggers appeared in her hands.

"Bloodthirsty little devil, aren't you?'' said the spacer. ''Ah, the simple enthusiasms of the young.''

A barefoot man in blue shorts of coarse-woven plastic and

nothing else grinned and raised a hatchet as he approached Kiril. A dirty bandanna was tied around his brow. "You don't get away this time, Kiril," he said.

"Come on," she urged, "I'll carve you just like I did your brother last year, you *schpurtzh*." The man whitened, then darted for her. He came to a sudden halt when the spacer trained the laser between his eyes. With the thump gun in his other hand, he menaced the rest. Even a crowd of thirty or more can lose its enthusiasm for blood with the realization that ten or more could die in seconds. Then the knowledge that Pao Lin might kill them all returned and they began to close in again. Movement stopped when a shadow passed over the crowd.

Kiril looked up. There was an atmosphere craft overhead. Two figures dropped from it without grav belts, even though the craft hovered at least fifteen meters up. Then they landed and stood flanking Kiril and the spacer. The mob stood paralyzed at the sight of them.

Kiril had never seen a Viver before, but she had heard of them; once human, their race had been genetically manipulated in the past to produce a creature so rugged and ferocious that it could survive under most circumstances. Covered with natural armor, provided with natural weapons, and possessing preternatural fighting savvy, a military armored vehicle was considered to be no match for a Viver. And here were two of them.

For a few seconds nobody moved. Then someone raised a slug gun and fired. There was a high-pitched crack as the pellet struck one of the Vivers on his protective chitin, followed by a hum as it ricocheted off. Then the Vivers were in the midst of the crowd. Their moves were so quick and powerful that their assailants had no time even to get out of the way, much less to fight back.

A backhanded blow from one of the Vivers felled three men, and he removed two more with a roundhouse kick of his bone-tipped foot before the first three even had time to fall. The other Viver rushed through the crowd, punching methodically with his spiked knuckles. He turned and worked his way back, striking with elbows and knees. Each blow landed effectively, and each was accompanied by a clearly audible sound of snapping bone.

It was too much for the mob. Those who could, turned and

ran. The brief whirlwind of action had lasted no more than ten seconds, but Kiril estimated that there were at least eighteen men sprawled moaning on the square. The átmosphere craft settled to the pavement and a small, mustachioed man at the controls signaled frantically for them to get in. As they climbed aboard, the spacers on the steps of the Spacer's Hall gave them a round of polite applause.

"Come on," said the big spacer, hauling Kiril over the side of the craft and piling after. The Vivers were already in place, and as she fell sprawling into the bottom of the AC, Kiril had only one thought: Maybe she was going to live after all!

"We'll be in trouble now," said the pilot. "The skipper's not going to like accounting to the authorities for a bunch of corpses."

"Nobody killed," said one of the Vivers. "Skipper says no killing, being a soft and irrational spoilsport. We did not use our talons or spurs." By way of demonstration, the Viver spread his fingers under Kiril's face and unsheathed five razor-edged, two-inch claws from their tips. From a bump on the back of his leg, just above the ankle and resembling a horse's fetlock, a seven-inch spur shot out. Kiril's stomach contracted at the sight, and she was not easily intimidated. For his entire seven-foot length the Viver was concentrated death.

At the field the pilot cut his speed. No one would follow them here. A spaceport was a planet's lifeline to the rest of the settled worlds. On many planets, spaceports and their occupants enjoyed a status of near-immunity. They flew past a line of tall ships owned by major companies, then slowed as they reached a small, battered freighter. The pilot eased the AC into its port, and Kiril's stomach did a flip-flop as the ship's grav field took hold and "vertical" became "horizontal."

A woman in an old, braided jacket and peaked cap glared at them as she chewed on an unlit Sirius V cigar.

"What have you done this time, Torwald? I send you into town to see about some supplies, and next thing I know you've got a riot going and you're calling for reinforcements."

"I was in the Gambler's Warren and—"

"Just what were you doing in the Warren? Can't I send you on a simple job without you exercising your taste for low company?"

"The Warren's a good place to pick up gear cheap. Anyway, I stepped out of a shed and this kid ran right into me. She was being chased by a goon with a thump gun. I couldn't just let her be killed—"

"Is this a girl?" The speaker was a tall, slender man who had entered the port through a door behind the skipper. His skin was pale but his hair and eyes were black as space. He leaned down and examined Kiril with his hands on his knees. "Faith, I believe you're right, though it's hard to tell, the kid being so skinny and all, and carrying so much dirt."

"You're looking for glamor, you gotta go uptown for it, you dumb *schturpter*!" Kiril spat.

"Such language," said the black-haired man, shaking his head in mock dismay, "and after we saved your life and all."

"Stow it, Finn," said the skipper. "Let's assemble all hands and figure out what kind of jam we're in." She touched a button on her belt and a quiet beeping sounded through the ship.

The spacer called Torwald guided Kiril out of the dock and into a passageway, then forward, toward the ship's nose. The passageway became a catwalk through a cavernous, empty hold. Then it became a floor once more as they entered another passage in the forward part of the ship. They went up a companionway to an upper deck and entered a large room with a long table in its center. Around the table sat a motley collection of crew members. The skipper gestured for Kiril to take an empty chair. Kiril sat and surveyed the company.

"First off," said the skipper, "I'm Captain HaLevy, skipper of the *Space Angel*. What's your name?"

"Kiril." She said it sullenly, as if this were a police interrogation.

"Why were you being chased?"

"Pao Lin wants me dead."

"You seem very young to have earned such antipathy," said an elderly, bright-eyed man. "Oh, excuse me, I'm Bert Sims, cargo chief."

She shrugged. "Young or old, it's all the same to Pao Lin. Cross him and you die."

"What did you do to him?" The questioner was a huge black man, as wide and heavy as Khan. He wore a mate's insignia on his collar.

"I was supposed to deliver a day's takings from a dope house to his collector. I kept half."

"Why'd you do that, knowing you'd be killed for it?" asked Torwald.

"I thought I could buy a passage out of this hole before Pao Lin caught on to the shortage. I picked the wrong time for it. Pao Lin was running a check on his collector and found out what I'd done. He posted men at all the ticket offices and put out the word on me. Just to make sure, he sent Khan. I gave the money to a pusher to give back, but that meant nothing. I stole from Pao Lin, so I have to be chopped."

"Do you have a family?" asked the skipper.

"No. I was brought here with a shipload of war refugees when I was little. They dumped me here in a camp, then the state got tired of paying for the camp and closed it down. I guess I was about nine then."

"Where were you before that?" asked Bert.

"Mao Zedong, but it was just another camp there. Before that . . ." She tried to remember, but she had not thought about this in a long time. All she could call back was a vague memory of a huge ship's hold packed with people. There was a terrible stench and screams of pain. "I don't know, another ship. I sort of remember somebody dying. Maybe it was my mother. I'm not sure."

"And what have you been doing since?" Bert asked.

"Picking up a living, scavenging, running errands for people."

"Thieving?" asked Torwald.

"Like I said, picking up a living. I'd steer marks to the gambling joints, watch for the police on other people's jobs, things like that."

"Rough life for a kid," said the black-haired man. "Oh, I'm Finn Cavanaugh, the navigator."

"How long since you've eaten?" asked a stunningly beautiful, blond woman.

"A couple of days, I guess. I think I had some soup the day before the trouble started." She could feel that their suspicion was dropping away as they looked at one another grimly.

"God, what the War's done," the skipper muttered to herself, shaking her head.

"Tor," said the blond woman, "fix Kiril something to eat. Make it light, her stomach probably won't tolerate much. Meanwhile, I'm going to give her a med exam. Nancy, bring some of your clothes. You're the only one close to her size." This last was addressed to a tiny, almond-eyed woman who had been sitting as still as a bronze statue throughout the meeting. She signified assent with a tiny nod. "Come along with me, dear," said the blond woman. She took Kiril's hand and led her out of the mess room. Kiril was a little shaky and lightheaded with fatigue, hunger, and relief. She was still on her guard, but beginning to feel a faint glimmering of hope, and hope was something she thought she had suppressed years ago.

"I'm Michelle LeBlanc, med officer," said the blonde. "Call me Michelle. Except for the skipper, we're on a first-name basis in this ship." Just forward of the hold Michelle stopped her at a door which bore a stylized emblem of a serpent wound around a staff. Inside were an examining table and a profusion of instruments, and Kiril could only guess at their function.

"First I'll have to give you a physical exam," Michelle said. "Go ahead and take off your clothes."

"Hey, what is this?" Kiril asked suspiciously.

"Don't you know it's all right to undress for a doctor?" Michelle said, amused.

"I've never seen a doctor before."

"Well, I can't examine you unless you do." The woman smiled winningly, but Kiril didn't trust smiles. The feeling she always had about such things told Kiril that the woman meant her well, but life had taught her to pay more attention to feelings of threat than to those of benevolence.

"Okay," she said at last, "I guess it's your ship." Just now she was willing to do almost anything to avoid leaving the ship. Almost. She unfastened her ragged coverall and slid out of it, sitting on a low table and pulling the filthy garment off over her bare feet. She was wearing the thin daggers strapped to both forearms.

"You'll have to take those off before I can take readings," said Michelle, as if such accoutrements were the most ordinary thing in the world. "You're safe here, Kiril," she added gently.

Kiril took off the knives and placed them on a shelf. Michelle attached tiny instruments to Kiril's wrists, chest, back, and forehead. She then proceeded to poke, prod, and pry with a businesslike forthrightness.

"Hey, what's that for? What are you doing?" Kiril was indignant. Michelle was examining her in places she was not used to having handled.

"Almost through," said Michelle. She began to unfasten her devices. "Now, step into that booth." She pointed to a transparent door in a wall. Kiril slid the door open and stepped inside. The chamber was barely large enough to turn around in.

"Don't be frightened," said Michelle, sliding the door shut. "It's just a medicinal bath. I know it's something different in your experience, but it's good for you."

Kiril started as a thick foam began rising in the booth. It had a harsh, astringent sting to it, and it kept rising. She was beginning to panic when it stopped short at her chin.

"Duck your head under and stay down as long as you can. Keep your eyes shut while you're under. Do that several times."

Kiril held her breath and closed her eyes. Screwing up her courage, she ducked. Immediately, she could feel the foamy stuff scrubbing at her scalp. "Different" was no adequate word for it. A bucket of cold water had been her only experience of bathing in Civis Astra. The stinging stopped and she could feel her pores opening. It began to feel good. Eventually the foam receded and she stepped from the booth. Michelle wrapped her in a huge, heated towel. It was the softest fabric she had ever felt. There was a knocking at the door.

"It's me, Nancy." The door opened and the woman entered, carrying a pile of clothes.

"This is Nancy Wu," said Michelle, "communications officer."

"How's the patient?" Nancy asked.

"Poor condition, physically. She's sixteen, but her physical development is that of a thirteen-year-old. That's mainly a result of malnutrition. Good food will clear it up, plus I'll put her on a hormone treatment. She's got enough problems to keep me busy for quite a while, but nothing that won't respond to treatment. Actually, it's kind of nice having a patient again. I don't have enough to do around here anyway."

The comm officer left and Kiril tried on the clothes. The coverall was baggy on her thin frame. She studied Michelle with curiosity.

"Why are you looking at me?" asked Michelle.

"I can't figure you. In Civis Astra a woman with your looks would belong to a big K'ang leader, or maybe some polit. Same with that other woman, Nancy. You two *work* on this ship, just like the rest?"

"That's right. Nancy handles communications, though she's not very communicative personally. I handle the medical department and see to everybody's health. Plus, Torwald and I take turns as ship's cook."

"You mean that big *schturtzl* with the gun cooks?" The idea strained Kiril's credulity.

"He's a man of many talents. His official capacity is quartermaster—he sees to equipment and supplies, but he's also a gourmet chef." Kiril didn't understand this. Food to her was fuel, nothing more. "Speaking of which," Michelle continued, "let's see if that food's ready." She guided Kiril back to the mess room again. Kiril sat at the table and Torwald put a tray in front of her. There was a soup and a few light, solid items.

"Eat this slowly, beginning with the soup," said Torwald. "We'll have to increase your intake gradually. I was a POW in the quarries on Signet during the War. I didn't look much better than you when I got liberated. The navy gave us as much as we could eat, and we all got sick, so take it slow."

Kiril began to spoon up the soup. It was delicious, and she had to fight the urge to bolt it and the rest. Food had always been something to eat as fast as possible, before someone else took it away from her.

"You all act as if I was going to stay here." She looked at them suspiciously. "Why's that?"

"Well," said Torwald, "you can't go back there, you'd just be killed. So, you stay with the ship."

"But I told you, I don't have the money anymore. I can't pay for a passage."

"Then you can work for it," Michelle said. "It happens that our last ship's boy left us a while back. He outgrew the job, so we have an empty berth. How would you like to be ship's girl?"

Kiril looked at her incredulously. "You mean I can stay until you reach another planet?"

"You can stay as long as you like," said Torwald. "Stay until you outgrow it, as long as you do your job. How about it?"

"Are you kidding? I'd do anything to get out of this sink." She paused. "Well, almost anything," she amended.

The skipper came in, carrying a flimsy printout sheet. "I've been talking with Port Authority. Seems a local 'businessman' named Pao Lin claims we're harboring a fugitive."

Kiril sat in her chair, paralyzed. The fear she had almost discarded came rushing back in full force. "Are you gonna let them take me?" Her words were edged with panic.

"No, of course not," said the skipper. "Just finish eating. The port people said that it'd take days for him to process enough red tape to extradite Kiril from the port area. They also say that Pao Lin is the biggest crook in the city and it's a pity we didn't let the Vivers kill all his men."

"Told you," said K'Stin, the taller of the two Vivers. The skipper looked at him with disgust.

"Since you're staying," Michelle said, "you might as well get to know people. Let's see, you've met Torwald and Nancy and Bert and Finn. That's Ham Sylvester over there. He's mate." The huge black man grinned and waved. "That's Achmed with the mustache, he piloted the AC that picked you up. Achmed's the engineer. That's his assistant sitting next to him. His name's Lafayette." The last named was a young man, perhaps nineteen or a little older. He had curly hair and a rakish look.

"The two Vivers are K'Stin and B'Shant. Don't bother trying to talk to B'Shant. K'Stin's his senior and always has first say." Kiril couldn't imagine wanting to talk to either of them. They were the most fearsome-looking creatures she had ever seen outside of a nightmare.

"Hello, are you going to be traveling with us?" The voice came from somewhere around Kiril's elbow, and she looked down. She then jumped nearly into the middle of the table. In the canals around Civis Astra there was a small creature called a crab, named for a resemblance to an Earth creature. The voice had come from something resembling a crab, only this one was about two feet high and four feet wide.

"What's that thing?" she yelled.

"That's just Homer," said the skipper. "He's the first intelligent alien ever discovered. He hitched a ride with us a while back and just sort of stayed. He's a poet."

"Vivers! Talking crabs! What kind of ship is this? Are you pirates or smugglers or something?"

"No," said the skipper, "just ordinary tramp freighters, moderately honest and usually broke. Now," she continued, "to our next order of business. When I checked with the port people about Kiril, here, they'd just received this message for us. It's from Earth High Command, ordering us to return to Earth, severing all contracts if necessary."

"How can they do that, and why?" asked Finn.

"I don't know why," the skipper said, "but as to how, it's under the old wartime Emergency Seizure Act. For all practical purposes we've been called back into the navy."

"Don't we ever get a break?" Torwald complained. "Why do we have to play footsie with those clowns?"

"Because they'll revoke our license if we don't," said the skipper. "We might as well go see what's on their minds. Liftoff in an hour. Kiril, if you've finished eating, come on up to the bridge."

Kiril still felt hungry but thought she had better heed Torwald's advice about taking it easy on the food. She got up and followed the skipper from the mess room all the way forward. The skipper opened a door and they stepped into a big room lined with control consoles. The skipper touched a plate on one of the consoles, and a thin, flexible strip of gold-colored metal was ejected.

"This is a spacer's bracelet," said the skipper, clipping the band around Kiril's left wrist, just below the dagger. "It will contain all the information regarding your service as a spacer. Once per ship-month you'll turn it in to me to have it updated. You're now Probationary Spacer, Second Class, aboard the good ship *Space Angel*." The skipper smiled for the first time, obviously an unaccustomed expression. "Glad to have you aboard, Kiril." Kiril didn't know quite what to say, so she said nothing, dropping her eyes to stare at the bracelet. The skipper took her arm and steered her back toward the mess room, which seemed to be the focal point of collective ship life.

"Lafayette," said the skipper, "show Kiril her quarters."

"Aye aye, Skipper," said the young man. "Come on, kid." He led Kiril back almost the whole length of the ship. "Your cabin's just abaft the main hold."

"Abaft?" said Kiril, mystified.

"That means behind. Forward means in front of." He pointed to a door. "That's a hatch, and that down there is the deck, not the floor. A stair is a companionway, and this," he slapped a wall, "is the bulkhead."

"Why does everything have a different name?"

"Tor says that when the first caveman paddled a log across water, he renamed everything on it so nobody would think he was a landsman. We carry on the tradition in space. Here you are, kid." He opened a door—Kiril corrected her thought—a hatch. Lafayette took her arm to guide her in, then froze when she whirled and laid a knife across his neck, just below the ear.

"Hands off!" she hissed. "I'll take orders and I'll do any job I'm told to, but you and the other men don't lay a hand on me, that clear?"

"Uh, extremely clear—pellucid, so to speak. Would you mind putting that blade up? Thank you. You weren't kidding about being from a rough neighborhood, were you?"

"Not hardly," Kiril said, going inside.

The cabin was about four paces long by three wide. Folded against a bulkhead were a bunk, a small desk, and a chair. There were some shelves, a sink, and a mirror.

"Who do I share this with?" Kiril asked.

"Nobody. It's all yours."

Kiril was awed, but tried not to show it. In Civis Astra a room this size would have housed a family of seven or eight. Even so, she had never been lucky enough to live in one. She had always slept in doorways, abandoned cellars, packing crates, anything that would keep off bad weather.

"We'll be lifting in a few minutes," said Lafayette. "Lower your bunk and strap in." He showed her how to release the catch holding the bunk in an upright position, and demonstrated how to fasten the straps. Then he went to his own cabin, across the passageway. Only when he was out of the cabin and the hatch securely locked did she get into the bunk and strap in.

A faint vibration started, then a slow, directionless pressure.

Both intensified, but did not become disturbing. After two or three minutes both halted abruptly and a feeling of weightlessness took their place. Then the feeling of gravity returned and a bong sounded in the intercom speaker.

"All hands unfasten, we're in free space." It was Ham's voice, coming over the intercom. Kiril loosened the straps and sat up. The bunk was uncomfortably soft and springy. She looked around more closely. There was a small bulb set in a recess in the bulkhead above her bunk. She touched a plate below it and a light came on. There were old clips on the bulkhead where former occupants had hung pictures or some such. She wondered briefly who they might have been. There was a knock at the hatch.

"Who is it?" Kiril called, hands going instinctively to her dagger hilts.

"It's Michelle." Kiril opened the hatch. Michelle was standing outside, holding a pile of white cloth and a cushion. "I've brought your linen," she said.

"Linen?"

"The cloth stuff that goes on the bunk. And a pillow."

"Oh, ah, thanks." Kiril was embarrassed that she wasn't sure what to do with the stuff, but Michelle walked past her and began making up the bunk, moving slowly so that Kiril could follow her actions.

"Michelle," Kiril asked, "what's this business about being called into the navy and having to go back to Earth without even a cargo?"

"No telling till we get there. This ship was in a peculiar situation a while back. We were forced to go to the center of the galaxy, thousands of times farther than humans have ever been before. That was when we got Homer. You mean you've never heard of the *Space Angel*? I thought the story had reached every corner of human-occupied space by now."

"I think I heard some spacers in the houses talking about it lately. I never paid much attention. Never thought I'd be spacing."

"I suppose you had other worries. Well, like it or not, you're a spacer now. You'll hear all about it on the way back to Earth, till you're sick of it. Torwald and Finn are the gabbiest braggarts you've ever met, and they're teaching Lafayette bad habits.

Don't believe too much of what they say. I don't doubt that our summons is somehow connected with that episode. Earth government never paid any attention to the *Angel* before. Nowadays we can't make a trip back there without some sort of complication.

"Look, you're pretty exhausted. By ship time, this is night. Why don't you try to get some sleep? There'll be plenty of time tomorrow for you to start learning your duties."

Suddenly Kiril was aware of just how exhausted she was. Too much had happened in too short a time. "Thanks. I could use some sleep."

"I'll see you tomorrow, then. Ham and Bert have bridge watch tonight until second night shift, then Finn and Nancy take over. You'll be assigned a watch later."

Michelle left and Kiril locked the hatch, then undressed and lay down on the bunk, shoving her daggers beneath the pillow. She had trouble getting comfortable. The bunk was so soft, and the pillow elevated her head at an unaccustomed angle. She tossed and twisted, finally hauling the mattress off the bunk and putting it on the deck. With that much solidity it seemed more familiar. It wasn't enough. She next discarded the pillow and set her daggers on the mattress beside her. That was better. She rested her head on a bent arm, put her free hand on a dagger hilt, and fell into a nervous, fitful sleep.

2

There was a bleep from the intercom. "Morning watch. All hands to the galley for breakfast or I'll throw it to the hogs." It was Michelle's voice. Kiril got up, yawning and stretching. Even on the floor—the deck, she reminded herself—the thin mattress had been soft enough to leave her stiff and sore after a few hours of restless sleep.

She went to the tiny sink and splashed cold water in her face, then washed in hot water, reveling in the luxury. She studied herself in the mirror. She had never really looked at her own face before, and she wasn't sure that she liked it much. Her dark-blond hair had always been kept trimmed as short as possible, so that she couldn't be grabbed by it. Below the hairline her face was thin and finely drawn, dominated by huge, almost spectral gray eyes. The skin, lightly dusted with freckles, was stretched so tight across the delicate bones that she looked emaciated. Well, maybe regular meals would fix that.

She realized that, for the first time in her life, she was thinking about her looks, as if they really mattered. She decided that the presence of women as striking as Michelle and Nancy was making her conscious of her own plainness.

Satisfied that she didn't look too disgraceful, Kiril went in search of the galley. Now that she had more time and was less confused, she took the opportunity to examine her new home. Her first home, to be precise. She might as well start thinking of it that way. It looked like she wasn't going to be anywhere else for a while.

From her cabin hatch she turned right and walked out onto the catwalk that ran through the center of the hold. The hold itself was a cavernous, cylindrical chamber, now totally empty. At intervals around its circumference Kiril could see the big hatches that were used for loading and unloading it. Immediately past the hold was a hatch opening onto the passageway labeled Cargo Crane. Kiril figured out the words quickly, but a hatch on the opposite side of the passage gave her some trouble: Hydroponics. She spelled the word out to herself, her lips forming the sound of the letters, but still it made no sense. Overcome by curiosity, she glanced up and down the passageway. Assured that nobody was watching, she gingerly opened the hatch. What she saw inside was a room full of plants, all floating in long baths of nutrient solutions. Puzzled, she pulled her head out and closed the hatch.

The ship was old, she could see that. The bulkheads lining the passageway and even the ceiling overhead were covered with a network of deep scratches, still visible under the paint. She didn't know much about ships, but she had been to the port enough times, and heard enough spacer's talk, to know that ships like this hadn't been built in a couple of generations.

Torwald stepped from a cabin into the passageway and spotted Kiril. "You lost?" he asked.

"Just taking my time," she said, defensively. "What are those scratches all over everything?"

"This is an old ship. She was built before the grav field was standard. In those days spacers wore magnetic plates on their boots. The plates made the scratches. No up or down on a ship in space in those days."

"Must have felt funny."

"Sometimes I wish the field hadn't been invented. I think it must have made for a more intimate relation between spacer and ship when there was no gravity.'' He stroked the battered bulkhead affectionately.

''Yeah, I guess so.'' Kiril had no idea what he was talking about. She decided Torwald was a little weird, like most spacers. He left her at the galley hatch. Inside, she found that most of the crew had eaten and gone.

''You're late,'' said Michelle. She and Bert were the room's only inhabitants. ''Don't worry, I saved something for you. We'll still keep it light.'' She set out a plate of food. Kiril wasn't sure what it was, but it smelled good. There was somewhat more solid fare than in her dinner the night before. She tore into it.

''I was looking around,'' Kiril said. ''I won't be late again.''

''You'll know your way around pretty soon,'' Bert said.

''What's the room full of plants? Hydro something or other.''

''Hydroponics,'' said Bert, immediately shifting into pedantic mode. ''That's where we grow vegetable matter to take up the carbon dioxide in our air and produce oxygen. Many of these plants have been specially gene-tailored for just this purpose. It also provides fresh vegetables to supplement our rations and helps to recycle some wastes. Besides, it's more homey to have growing plants around. I take it that you can read, then?''

''Some,'' Kiril said around a mouthful of food. ''There was an old guy in Civis Astra. He was sick with something and needed drugs to kill the pain. I used to hustle the stuff for him, and in return he taught me a little reading and numbers. He died about a year ago, I guess. I really missed him.''

''Well,'' said Bert, ''we'll see if we can't improve your education a bit. You can begin your duties by helping me sort out the cargo records, and you'll learn a few things in the process. How does that sound Michelle, my sweet?''

''Fine,'' Michelle said. ''She's on light duties until I say otherwise. Here, Kiril, drink this.'' Michelle handed Kiril a tall beaker filled with a thick, foamy liquid.

''It's basically milk and sugars, with a couple of eggs and a lot of vitamins and nutrients. It'll help you put on weight and clear up your deficiency conditions. Drink it slowly, over the next hour or so. From now on you'll drink three liters of this each day until I discontinue it.'' Kiril sipped at the stuff gingerly. It was intensely sweet, but not unpleasant. It was a temptation to drink it fast. She had never been able to get enough of sweets before, and her body craved sugar.

When she finished eating, Kiril followed Bert to his cabin-office combination on the lower level. The two small rooms were crammed with the souvenirs of a long life spent in space, but the area devoted to business was perfectly neat and orderly. While Bert called up his records on a little desk console, Kiril examined odd bits of rock, shells, plates containing three-dimensional images of alien landscapes and seascapes, odd fabrics and jewels. ''This place looks like one of those curio shops for spacers.''

''These aren't just for looks,'' said Bert, picking up a cube of transparent glassite in which was embedded something that looked like a lobster with wings. ''Every item here has a story behind it, some connection with my life and travels. I've never felt comfortable with keeping a diary. It feels too much like talking to myself. This is my substitute.'' The screen lit up with columns of figures and words. ''Now, my dear, you are going to learn the mysteries of bills of lading.''

Kiril leaned over his shoulder, sipping at her beaker and studying the screen.

''These are the food troughs,'' Michelle said. They were in the hydroponics room, amid high humidity and the smell of growing things. This was a wonderland. Civis Astra had had no parks and Kiril had never been into the countryside. She had seen few plants in her life except for weeds growing in vacant lots and occasional decorative plants growing high on the balconies of rich peoples' housing.

In a long, transparent trough, dozens of small, green apples grew from a single, thin stem which ran along the bottom of the trough. ''A couple of centuries ago,'' Michelle told her, ''we'd have needed a whole tree to grow these. Master stem fruits and vegetables were developed around the time of early space settlement. People just never got used to fully artificial food. In an HP room this small we can't grow enough to feed everybody, but it makes a nice supplement for preserved foods.''

The last few weeks had been like this: Kiril helped one crewperson after another, getting instruction in most of the ship's jobs and other, related subjects. Bert polished up her reading, Nancy and Finn gave her progressively more advanced mathematical instruction. Torwald versed her on the ins and outs of a spacer's existence, about which he seemed to know more than any honest spacer should. He was, as advertised, a self-proclaimed expert on everything. The odd thing was, he really seemed to be almost as knowledgeable as he said he was.

The only places where she wasn't receiving instruction were the bridge and the engine room. She would need years more education and experience before she could begin to study for a bridge officer's job. The engine room, domain of Achmed and Lafayette, Michelle had ruled off limits as too subject to extremes of heat when under conventional drive, and the work to be done there too heavy.

"You think I lived in a controlled environment back on Thoth?" Kiril protested. She had been learning lots of new terms like that.

"I'm the doctor," Michelle answered, and that was that.

When they were far enough from Thoth's primary star to use the Whooppee drive, Michelle had Kiril endure the ordeal in the infirmary, strapped into a therapeutic chair and wired from toes to scalp. She would have gone through Whooppee transition with Kiril, but at that time she was in no better shape than anybody else.

The transition from "real" space to hyperspace by Whooppee drive was accompanied by physical convulsions as all bodily functions cut loose at once. Much worse, the convulsions were followed by several minutes of hallucinations; horrors dredged up from the most hidden recesses of the traveler's subconscious. It was the "Whooppee horrors" that caused many to swear off spacing forever. Kiril came through shaken but sound, with only a vague memory of unbearable terrors during the immeasurable time of transition. Michelle considered it a tribute to her psychological toughness and resiliency.

* * *

They emerged in real space in the void between the orbits of Jupiter and Saturn. They still had a long way to go to reach their destination in Earth orbit. As soon as Kiril was over her post-Whoopee shakiness, she went to the supply room to help Torwald with his scheduled inventory and maintenance: inspecting each piece of equipment on the storeroom's manifest and making sure that each was serviceable. They had been at this task for an hour when Finn stuck his head through the hatch.

"Torwald, my jewel, we have new orders: We're not to land on Earth after all, we're to rendezvous with navy station *Leyte*. She's orbiting off Luna just now."

"*Leyte?*" said Torwald, eyebrows shooting up. "You're sure?"

"Certain. Nancy picked up the signal as soon as we left hyper. It came by Priority One Secret beam." He paused dramatically to let it sink in.

"What's that?" Kiril asked.

"It's a beam that hasn't been used, to my knowledge, since the end of the War. How long before we get there?"

"Skipper says a couple of weeks. We were lucky with the alignment of the planets. Coming out where we did, it could have taken us eight weeks or more to reach Luna."

"I know about Earth," Kiril said, "but what's Luna?"

"Earth's moon," Torwald told her. "A barren hunk of rock with all its settlements underground. It's pretty from Earth, but not from close up."

"Sorry, m'love," Finn said to Kiril. "You won't get to see the fleshpots of Earth this trip, it seems."

"Suits me," Kiril said. "Cities've been nothing but a pain to me, anyway. I've had enough of them." She meant every word. The ship had come to mean safety and security to her. If she had her way, Kiril would never leave the ship for the rest of her life.

"You won't be missing much," Torwald assured her. "The cities there are mostly slums not much better than Civis Astra. Except for a few resorts in Africa and South America, the greenery is mostly gone. They even have to keep the atmosphere replenished with artificial systems."

"Even Ireland isn't very green any more," said Finn sadly.

"You two just wring my heart," said Kiril. "Almost the only

plants I ever saw in my life are down there in the HP room. If those are the only ones I ever see, I'll be happy.'' By now Kiril trusted both men, even liked them to a certain extent, but she wouldn't pass up a chance to needle Finn's Celtic sentimentality or Torwald's complacent expertise. Men had to be kept in their place.

She was down to one liter of the concentrated nutrient per day now. She had gained at least twenty pounds, but she still looked thin. She picked up her ever-present beaker and downed the last of it, making a face at the cloying sweetness. It hadn't taken long for the sugary taste to pall on her.

''Something very hush-hush is going on,'' Torwald said after Finn had left. ''And we're in the middle of it.''

''No kidding,'' said Kiril, touching the edge of a heavy jungle knife. She hefted the knife by its alumisteel handle. ''This thing has no balance at all. A good hand with a sticker could gut you in the time it took you to crank up for a cut. And it's too point-heavy to throw.''

''Don't be so relentlessly bloody-minded,'' said Torwald. ''It's a tool, primarily, not a weapon. For cutting brush and vines and stuff.''

''What're vines?''

''Stringy plants. I'll show you pictures sometime. And don't underestimate its capabilities as a weapon.'' He took the knife and held it dangling at his side. Suddenly the blade flashed out and Kiril felt the breeze of its passage by her ear. A tiny wisp of her hair drifted to the deck. She hadn't flinched or even blinked.

''Show-off,'' she snorted.

Kiril left the galley late. She had helped Michelle clean up, then had taken a pitcher of coffee up to the bridge for the two on watch. She had tried the coffee once and found it to be repellently bitter. The others, however, seemed to live on the awful stuff. She'd taken the empty pitcher back to the galley, rinsed it and put it away. They were still a few days from their destination, there was little to do at the moment, and everybody except Kiril and the watch had turned in, or so she thought.

As she closed the hatch to the galley and mess room, she heard an unfamiliar sound. It was so faint that it was almost subliminal, but her hearing was keener than most. Something about the sound tugged at her. It was coming from above, somewhere in the vicinity of the bridge. She went up the companionway and turned back down the narrow passage at the top. She could move as silently as a ghost when she wanted to, and the two on watch never noticed her. The sound was louder now. It was music, and it was the most beautiful thing she had ever heard. The music she was used to was the loud, abrasive noise played in the bars and houses where she had cleaned and run errands for meals. This was something entirely different. It was coming from Finn's navigation chamber.

Silently, she opened the hatch. The navigation chamber was empty, its lights out. The music was coming from somewhere beyond. She saw a vertical line of dim light at the far side of the chamber. It was coming from a hatch she had never noticed before. She crossed the chamber and put her eye to the crack between hatch and jamb. Beyond was a room, its deck carpeted and roofed with a transparent bubble. Through it shone a multitude of stars. It struck Kiril that she had been in space for weeks now and had never seen the stars except on the screens in the bridge and navigation chamber. The room she was looking into had no instruments or furnishings of any kind, but there were marks where fixtures had been removed. Nancy Wu was sitting cross-legged on the deck, and she was making the music.

Nancy held a stringed instrument to one shoulder, her cheek laid along its base and the fingers of her left hand magically manipulating the strings along its neck. Her other hand slid a long stick gracefully up and down, across the strings. The music tugged at Kiril's heart in a way she had never experienced before. At the same time, she felt she was intruding on something private, but she couldn't make herself turn away from the beautiful sounds. Nancy was the hardest of all the crew to talk to. She spoke briefly and to the point, always about the work at hand or instructions when she was teaching Kiril something. She never took part in the others' conversations. It struck Kiril that she was hearing Nancy talk for the first time.

Nancy swayed where she sat, in time with the music. Once she half turned, her face slightly toward the hatch, and Kiril stepped back into the dimness. She saw that it was unnecessary;

Nancy's eyes were shut and she was oblivious to all around her. Reluctantly, Kiril backed away and left the navigation chamber. Back in her bunk the image she had last seen stayed with her: It was Nancy Wu's face, rapt with the spell of her music, bright tears making long tracks from her closed eyes down her cheeks.

Navy station *Leyte* was a small facility; a wheel-shaped main pod surrounded by floating docks for servicing naval vessels up to medium cruiser size. There were no cruisers there now. The *Angel*'s crew could see that much on the main screen. There were only two ships visible, and both were much too large for the station's docks.

"What are those two ships?" asked Kiril. She was disturbed at her shipmates' alarmed expressions. The entire crew were crammed into the ship's bridge, trying to second-guess their fate.

"One is a Navy Task Force Command Ship," said Michelle, who stood next to her. "They've been demobilized since the War ended—too expensive to run. They must've taken this one out of mothballs. The other I don't recognize. It has Satsuma markings, but it's bigger than any line ship I've ever seen. You recognize it, Skipper?"·

"I've just seen pictures," said the skipper. "It's got to be Satsuma's new Supernova, the ship that's going to replace the old Class Ones. The Supernova wasn't supposed to be spacing for another couple of years, though—still in the testing stage."

"'Curiouser and curiouser,'" Bert said.

"If it's Satsuma's only working Supernova, there's only one man they'd put in command of it," said the skipper, her face set in a vicious scowl.

"Izquierda," said Ham. Kiril glanced at him. His big moon face was as bland as ever, but she knew rage when she heard it.

"Hey, now, the War's over," Torwald said. Obviously he didn't like the tone of his commanders.

"Well, lookee here," said Finn. He had zeroed a screen on the nose of the naval vessel. The closeup displayed a plaque of bright gold, bearing a triangle of three silver comets.

"An Admiral of the Gold," Torwald said. He was impressed. "They've never had one of those in peacetime. Think there's a war on?"

"It's got to be Nagamitsu," said the skipper. "They must have called him out of retirement." Even Kiril knew that name. Nagamitsu had been the most illustrious commander of the War. Toward the end he had been appointed Grand Admiral of Allied Fleets, the only man ever so honored.

"What *is* this?" asked Michelle, of nobody in particular.

"We're about to find out," the skipper said.

"Maybe there will be fighting!" K'Stin said eagerly. Bert had told Kiril that the Viver race was so obsessed with survival, both personal and racial, that they usually avoided other peoples' fights. These two, however, were in their testing period, an unspecified number of years when young Vivers wandered, seeking adventures and wars to take part in, to prove themselves fit to propagate their species.

A face appeared on the ship-to-ship screen, accompanied by a voice. Face and voice belonged to a middle-aged woman wearing a navy uniform. At her collar was the insignia of the Security Corps.

"Freighter *Space Angel:* You will dock in the main bay of the Task Force Command Ship *Sic Semper Tyrannis.* You will attempt no communication with any personnel except those wearing Special Security tabs." She touched her own; a disk attached to the collar of her uniform.

"By authority of Grand Admiral Nagamitsu, acting in direct subordination to the Security Council under the State Emergency Military Bypass Act."

Torwald gave a low whistle. "The government's cut out the whole military superstructure." He added with satisfaction: "We were right about Nagamitsu."

"Please place your ship's controls on remote," said the navy woman. "Docking Authority will guide your ship to its berth." Despite her dry, official tone, the woman managed to give a slightly ironic twist to the word "ship."

"*Sic Semper Tyrannis,*" mused the skipper, lighting one of her noxious cigars. "I served in that old bucket when I was a cadet. We called her the *Sick Tyrant* in those days."

"Are we actually going inside that thing?" asked Kiril. "It can't be that big!"

"One of those bays will hold six ships the size of the *Angel*," said the skipper. "A TFCS is really a free-roving space station." The bay entrance loomed ever larger in the screen. "Look at that bay," she continued. "Completely empty. I can't believe they're staging all this for us. Come on, let's go to the gangway and see what this is all about."

"This is most exciting," said Homer. "I foresee fine epic material in the offing." Kiril patted his shell. The crustacean had been teaching her a variety of subjects. In spite of, or perhaps because of, his alien appearance, she found it much easier to trust Homer than to trust the humans. They were now fast friends.

"Just what I need," Kiril said ruefully, "a role in a talking crab's poem."

Kiril stood nervously between Nancy and Lafayette. Her life aboard ship had been agreeably simple and comfortable, and now all was uncertain and insecure again. This situation seemed to overwhelm even her shipmates, and that disturbed her.

"Now, keep in mind," Lafayette urged in a whisper, "you'll get a lot of nasty looks from navy people. Just remember you're a free freighter and pretend they're too low for you to even notice. The line people will be even worse, but pay them no attention." The animosity between the free freighters and the lines was deep and ancient. There was only slightly less hostility toward the navy. Most of the older members of the *Angel*'s crew had at one time served in the navy, but only as wartime duty. Independent freighters were an unruly breed, and hated the regimentation that prevailed in navy and line ships.

When the signal came, the skipper cycled the hatch open. Outside, on the vast deck, was an honor guard of Spacer Marines. The marines were drawn up in a double line facing each other, beam rifles at present arms. They were powerful men in shiny boots and white gloves, and wearing gleaming, black helmets. Of all the services, only Spacer Marines were permitted to handle energy small arms aboard a ship in space. At the far end of the double rank was an officer in full-dress uniform, complete with cape and ceremonial sword.

"They only wear those silly outfits on diplomatic assignments,'' Torwald muttered.

"Shut up, Tor,'' said the skipper. "All right, crew, let's show 'em who we are.''

The *Space Angel*'s crew set off down the ramp in no particular order, vests and shirts unbuttoned, caps pushed back or shoved forward or canted to one side, deliberately exaggerating their slouch and sloppiness to spite the spit-and-polish marines. Homer was burbling one of his alien poems happily, delighted at the odd habits of humans. The towering Vivers eyed the marines with openly contemptuous amusement. A few of the marines, while perfectly motionless, could be seen to sweat.

The officer, while remaining quite correct, grew red about the ears. "Captain HaLevy?'' he asked, saluting smartly.

"That's right, sonny,'' she said. "What's up?''

"You shall be informed in good time. I am Major Martinaux.'' He was obviously too young to be a major, but by ancient custom, marine captains received the courtesy rank of major while serving aboard ship. There was only one captain in a naval vessel in space. "If you will come this way, please?''

"Do we have any choice?'' asked the skipper.

The young officer allowed himself the minutest smile of satisfaction. "None at all.'' The marines performed a precise facing movement, and the *Angel*'s crew tramped off between the two files. The skipper immediately stepped up next to the officer, on his right side. He looked distinctly nettled.

"The superior officer stands on the right,'' whispered Lafayette to Kiril. She nodded, beginning to enjoy this games-playing. It confirmed her long-held opinion that all spacers, military or civilian, had the minds of ten-year-olds, but she was determined not to let the team down. She looked at the intimidating marines with the same feigned, amused contempt as the others.

They left the immense landing bay and entered an elevator as large as the *Angel*'s hold. They got off at a landing marked with a complicated blue-and-white insignia. "Diplomatic Corps,'' said Torwald, in an I-told-you-so tone of voice. From the landing they trooped down a long corridor that was as high-ceilinged as a cathedral. Bay, elevator, and hall were military spare. All was plain, functional, Spartan. The marine guard came to a stomping halt before a huge double door. The officer presented himself to a small sensor plate set in one of the doors. There was a musical beep and the portals swung wide. They entered, leaving the honor guard outside.

Within the doors, it seemed like another ship. Here, all was luxury. They were in a suite furnished with exotic woods, leathers, furs, marbles, and metals, the finest materials of many far-flung worlds. Each fitting, furnishing, and decoration was a priceless work of art. Kiril gaped about her. To her, the frugal environs of the *Space Angel* had seemed the height of luxury. This was staggering. Nancy elbowed her in the ribs and she resumed her air of disdain.

"Nice place you got here," said the skipper, knocking an ash into a priceless tray carved from Spica ruby. "I don't think this suite was in this tub when I served in her. Let's see, that would've been about the time you were being toilet-trained, Major." Her pronunciation of his rank left no doubt as to her opinion of its validity.

"If you will wait here, Captain, you shall be met presently by persons authorized to discuss the situation." The officer whirled and stalked off in a furious huff, his back ramrod stiff.

"No action these days to knock the starch out of 'em," the skipper mused.

They flopped on the couches and hassocks and made themselves comfortable while awaiting the attentions of the powers-that-be. Homer began humming a Bach string quartet, which his multitudinous vocal chords could reproduce with astonishing fidelity.

Kiril sat in a chaise longue, feeling its softness yield perfectly to every angle of her still-bony body. The effect was unsettling, but she was sure that she could get to like it, given continued proximity.

A door opened and a man in civilian clothes bearing the badge of the Diplomatic Corps entered. He was short, fat, and gray-haired, and he smiled benignly as he offered his hand to the skipper.

"Ah, Captain HaLevy, welcome. I do apologize for the abrupt summons and the peremptory manner in which it was phrased. It was, however, a matter of state security. Ah, here is the admiral." Through another door came a taller man, broad and blocky, but carrying no surplus flesh. He wore a navy dress uniform, much plainer than the marine variety, with three silver comets blazing from each epaulet.

"I'm Nagamitsu," he said without preamble. "You people will be the officers and crew of *Space Angel*?" He glanced quickly over them. "Of course you are. Your pictures were everywhere a while back. And I've seen this remarkable being at a number of scientific functions." He smiled down at Homer.

"Honored to make your acquaintance, Admiral," said the skipper, sounding as if she meant it.

"Let's get down to business," said the admiral. "This gentleman is the honorable Winston Pierce of the Diplomatic Corps. Mr. Pierce, perhaps you had better begin."

"Well, ah, it seems that we are in for exciting times. First, a short while back the *Space Angel* returned from her unprecedented voyage to the center of the galaxy, in the process of which was proven once and for all that other intelligent life exists within our galaxy. Now, it seems, other Earth spacers have arrived at a similar discovery independently."

Everyone sat up straighter. Their own voyage had been involuntary; accomplished under the control of an unimaginably powerful being that took them far beyond the areas explored by humans. Intelligent aliens had never before been encountered in human-occupied space.

"Last year a merchant vessel, scouting new areas for exploitation, encountered an alien settlement. It was inhabited by a large colony of intelligent creatures. In accordance with Rule One, passed more than a century ago, he did not attempt communication, but restricted himself to taking images and readings, and refrained from any action which might be misinterpreted as hostile. Upon his return to Earth, the captain of the ship very wisely bound his crew to secrecy and informed only the superiors of his line whom he knew to have top security clearances. These, in turn, informed the Security Council."

"That's news of a high order, all right," said the skipper. "But just where do our humble selves come into all this?"

"The Council has decided that, as the only humans with any extensive dealings with intelligent alien beings in the past, your services in an advisory capacity might be of considerable value."

"And the rate of pay?" she asked.

"It shall be substantial. You will bear in mind, of course, that you will be serving the government."

"That government hasn't done much for us lately," said the skipper. "After our 'epochal journey,' as it was called, the government confiscated our whole cargo."

"For further study, of course. I might add that your cooperation in this matter could greatly facilitate the release of those items."

"Put that in writing and you have a ship," said the skipper. "Assuming, of course, that the rest of my crew agrees." She looked around. The rest gave reluctant nods. Kiril was a little puzzled at their attitude, but she left the question for later.

"Now," said the admiral, "let's show these people what little we know so far." He punched a button in the arm of his chair, and a man promptly appeared through a door. He appeared to be around thirty years old and he wore the uniform of the Satsuma Line, with the collar insignia of a captain in the Expeditionary Branch.

"This," said Nagamitsu, "is Mr. Ng, master of the *Hideyoshi*. It was his ship that discovered the aliens." Ng inclined his head slightly toward the *Angel*'s spacers. Behind him an entire half of the large room filled with pale green light. It was an immense holographic tank. Ng began his monologue in a dry tone which indicated that he had delivered it frequently of late.

"My ship was on an assignment to check out the system around D6835, a G-type in the Pleiades Sector. It was a standard system: four gas giants, six ice-and-rock balls, and two Earth-types, one of them so marginal as to exclude colonization short of finding really valuable and exploitable materials. Naturally, I turned my attention to the better Earth-type.

"I established orbit and instituted a scan. Immediately my instruments picked up a signal on a band not commonly used. I suspected a smuggler or pirate base and took suitable precautions to avoid being detected myself. My computer could make nothing of the signal after extended analysis, so I determined to make a reconnaissance."

"Kind of risky, wasn't it?" said Torwald.

"My ship is equipped with the armament customary for a line explorer," said Ng, with a touch of superiority, "and any such base could represent a threat to any ships of my line that might follow.

"I spotted the location of the signal's source. It was a rather large facility, much larger than any smuggler or pirate base would be. At first I thought it might be a base for a rival line, but after double-checking official records, I was sure that no legitimate concern had filed a claim anywhere in that system. I next considered the possibility of a secret military installation, but soon discarded that."

"They'd never have let you file a spacing plan for that system if that'd been the case," said Ham.

"Exactly," said Ng. "I could see that something peculiar was going on, to say the least. This is what I was watching through my screens." The holo tank showed a series of buildings as seen telescopically from space. They looked small, but there was no scale to judge them by. Their outlines were hazy, apparently from the intervening atmosphere. "I tried to get better resolution through computer enhancement, but was unable to. That should have tipped me off, but at the time the idea of alien settlements was still theoretical. This was, you understand, before news of the *Space Angel*'s feat had reached the sector where I was stationed." He favored the *Angel*'s crew with another, barely civil nod.

"While debating my next move, I saw this." In the tank a ship suddenly appeared from outside the viewer's range, headed for what was obviously a landing apron on the ground. All sat up straight, even Nagamitsu, who, Kiril thought, must have seen this holo many times before. The room erupted in muttering and exclamations from her shipmates. Kiril was no expert on spacecraft, but even she could see that this ship was not of any design produced by humans. It was a collection of spheres of varying sizes, arranged in an irregular circle and connected by a system of delicate struts. The whole thing was colored black.

"Can we get a close-up of that thing?" the skipper asked.

"Certainly," said Nagamitsu, "but you'll be disappointed." The strange craft froze in position and the viewer zoomed in. As the perspective shortened, the resolution got no clearer. Wavy, shimmering lines interposed to make every feature of the ship unclear and hazy. "As you can see, the ship, like the ground facility, employed a masking device, much like the one Mr. Ng used to avoid detection, but far more sophisticated. Please continue, Mr. Ng."

"There is little more. I saw instantly that not only was this ship not of human design, but it could not be made to land on a full-gravity planet by any stretch of human engineering. I knew that I had made a discovery of the utmost importance to humanity. What I had was maddeningly incomplete, and I wanted to try for more data, but Rule One is very specific on this question. Such data as I had, I sent out on subspace in case I shouldn't make it back, and I headed for home. That system requires an unusually great distance from the primary for the Whooppee drive to function, so I only made it back three months ago."

"Thank you, Mr. Ng," said Pierce. He turned to the *Angel*'s people. "Before we proceed further, have you any questions to ask Mr. Ng?"

"You referred to that place as a 'colony,'" said Torwald. "Is it certain that it isn't their native planet?"

"Absolutely," Ng said. "We did a standard scan of the planet, we took atmosphere and water samplings with remotes, all the usual procedures. We found no other settlements, not that that means a lot. For all we know, they might live underground. But the air and water of that world are absolutely unpolluted. Whoever built that ship had a long history of industrial development before they ever got into space, and it would show in the air and water, even if they had progressed to clean industry and energy thousands of years ago. That planet is pristine."

"How far from that little port did the masking effect reach?" the skipper asked.

"Approximately six hundred kilometers," Ng said. "It is far more powerful than anything we have. They could be hiding a lot down there."

"If there are no further questions," Pierce said. "Thank you, Mr. Ng." The Satsuma captain bowed and left the room.

"Who's going on this expedition?" the skipper asked.

"The Council debated that point for a long time," Pierce said. "Yourselves, of course, for the reasons already specified. The naval contingent, headed by Grand Admiral Nagamitsu, will represent the military. The diplomatic mission, which I shall be heading, shall also travel in this vessel. The civilian sector shall be represented by a large scientific contingent, traveling in the Satsuma vessel alongside."

"I was going to ask about that ship," said the skipper. "Why Satsuma?"

"The Council was, of course, anxious to maintain a complete separation of the military and civilian missions," Pierce said, "and also wished to impress upon the aliens our considerable technology, as well as our military might. The Satsuma Supernova, I'm sure you will agree, is the most spectacular of our civilian vessels, just as this TFCS is the most impressive in the navy."

"If they can make ships like the one we just saw, and land them on Earth-type planets," said Torwald, "they aren't likely to be impressed by anything we can show them."

"All levels of technological development needn't be equally advanced," said Pierce blandly. "They seem to have some kind of engineering new to us. They may well find our own space-going technology equally awesome."

"It will not have escaped your notice," Nagamitsu said, "that those people were using a masking device it is unlikely they would have dreamed up unless they've had experience of warfare. At some time in their history, posssibly recently, they've had good reason to mask their ships and facilities. We have to proceed as if warfare between our species were a possibility. They won't know that the TFCS is our largest and most powerful warship. If it doesn't strike them as all that impressive, we can always leave them with the speculation that maybe we have far more powerful vessels."

"Who's in command of the Supernova?" Ham asked casually.

"Ramon Izquierda," said Pierce. Kiril ignored Pierce and concentrated on Nagamitsu. His face revealed nothing, but something about him changed at mention of the name.

"The directors of Satsuma assured us that only Commander Izquierda could be entrusted with the Supernova," Nagamitsu said thinly. "It's still largely experimental, and they wouldn't have anybody else. The Council seems not to have been inclined to dispute with them."

"I see, " said the skipper grimly. "Are we going to have to ride in your hold for the whole trip?"

"I'm afraid so," said Nagamitsu. "Sorry, but you wouldn't be able to keep up with us to the edge of the system. If you wish, you may travel independently afterwards."

"Just as long as we don't have to travel in Izquierda's ship," said the skipper. The admiral seemed about to snap out a sharp retort, but Pierce stepped in to smooth things over.

"This evening we will be having a formal dinner for the ship's officers and the higher-ranking scientists and diplomatic personnel. Your entire ship's company is, of course, invited. You are, after all, interplanetary celebrities. Everyone would be *most* disappointed if you weren't there."

"That's real democratic of you," said the skipper. "Sure, we'll be there. Wouldn't miss it for anything."

They took their leave and made their way back to the *Angel*, this time without the marine guard. Inside they held a council.

"Skipper," said Achmed, "do you really buy all this stuff about us being valuable in an advisory capacity?"

"Not for a minute," she said. "They don't need us for this expedition. What do we know about these aliens? I can see them wanting Homer. He might have encountered them before, and if not, he could learn their language faster than any human. But the rest of us?" She looked around the cabin at her crew and snorted. "We wouldn't have much advice to give, and they wouldn't take it if we had."

"It's got to be Izquierda," said Ham. "He's behind it, somehow."

"I don't think old Nagamitsu likes this business of Izquierda being along," said Torwald.

"He hates him," said Kiril. "He'd like to see him dead."

"Huh? Why do you say that?" asked the skipper.

"Wasn't it obvious?" said Kiril, surprised. "Couldn't you tell from his voice and face?"

"Nope," said Ham succinctly. "Michelle, you think Kiril might be a sensitive?"

"I wouldn't be surprised. If she has even a latent capability, living where she did would bring it out as a survival mechanism."

"Excellent," said K'Stin, hearing every Viver's favorite word.

"Let's hope she has the talent," said the skipper. "Michelle, I want you to give her the best test series you can come up with. Kiril, from now on I want you with me whenever I have dealings with any of those people."

"Sure," Kiril said, confused, "but what's all this business with Izquierda? Why do you all hate him?"

"Back before he became one of the richest and most powerful men in known space," said the skipper, grim-faced, "he was a navy officer, at one time holding the position of commodore of a heavy squadron. He had the task of evacuating the trade station on Delta Orion Five. There were ten thousand civilians working that station, and a couple of thousand POW's in a camp. There were also seven big Satsuma freighters in port at the time."

"He was a stockholder in Satsuma even then," said Ham, taking up the tale. "Under navy regs, he was supposed to dump the cargoes of those freighters and use the cargo space to evacuate the civilians and prisoners. When a Triumvirate force was spotted heading for D.O. Five, he split the squadron and sent half to deal with the enemy. He kept the rest to act as convoy. The full squadron might have forced them to head for home, but Izquierda wasn't taking any chances. He let them be annihilated to buy him enough time to get those Satsuma ships off-planet, with their cargoes. He left the noncombatants to be wiped out by the Triumvirate ships. They sterilized the planet with torch bombs."

"He was court-martialed and cashiered from the service," continued the skipper. "He had great wealth and influence even then, or he would have been shot. Of course, Satsuma Line was agitating for him all the way. As it was, the trial was hushed up. Bad for civilian morale, the Council thought. He even bought enough influence with the government in the years after the War to have the dishonorable expulsion revoked. He even tried to have the trial records destroyed, but they were already in the Archives and even he couldn't touch them. I still have friends who keep me informed about him. He hates me with a real passion."

"Why?" Kiril asked.

"Because it was me that turned him in."

3

Kiril fretted as Nancy and Michelle stitched her into a dress of Nancy's that was not so large as to be out of the question. In the places where Kiril failed to fill out the dress, Michelle artfully took out the wrinkles with surgical plastiflesh.

"I want you to remember," cautioned Michelle, "this is a formal dinner, so be on your best behavior."

"Why? We weren't trying to be formal with those marines."

"That was different," Michelle said. "Martinets and bureaucrats have to be put firmly in their place. At an affair like this we have to be presentable, because they'll be expecting us to act like slobs. You understand?"

"I guess so," said Kiril doubtfully.

"The women will be paired with men," Michelle continued, "it's customary. The skipper with Ham, Torwald with me, Nancy with Finn, and you're paired with Lafayette. When we go into the dining room, he'll have to take your arm, so try to remember not to knife him."

"I don't know," said Kiril. "Old habits are hard to break."

"Give it a try, anyway," said Michelle.

When the dress fit to everyone's satisfaction, Nancy and Michelle set about applying Kiril's makeup. There was no way to make her face seem less hollow-cheeked, so it was decided to make that feature an asset. Kiril's face was dominated by her huge eyes, and Nancy cleverly accented the lids and lashes to make them even more dramatic. Her short hair had now grown long enough to set in a cap of tight ringlets.

When they were finished, Kiril surveyed the effect in a full-length holoviewer. She was stunned. Her face had changed from that of a Civis Astra guttersnipe to that of a civilized lady. The long, high-necked dress clung closely to her (occasionally artificial) contours, and its billowy sleeves concealed the twin daggers she still refused to part with. She was utterly changed, transfigured. Now, if she could just remember not to stab Lafayette when he touched her!

At the lock they met the others. Finn, Torwald, and Lafayette were wearing formal suits; short jackets with high standing collars heavily embroidered with gold and with matching embroidery on the sleeves, skintight trousers stuffed into high, shiny boots. Finn's outfit was black, Torwald's silvery gray, and Lafayette's bright scarlet. They all wore broad sashes and waist-length capes, and the two older men wore small, discreet copies of their military decorations pinned to their jackets, as was permitted for a diplomatic function.

"And I thought *I* looked changed!" Kiril commented.

"You'd be surprised what you'll find, rummaging through a spacer's bag," said Torwald. "And, may I add, Lafayette is going to be a much-envied man tonight." Kiril refused to blush: it wasn't her style.

Ham and the skipper arrived, both in full naval dress with the Reserve collar insignia. "What do you know?" said Finn. "It still fits after all these years." She favored him with a look that boded ill for his future duties.

"Where are Bert and Achmed?" Michelle asked.

"They've elected not to attend," said Torwald. "They're going to a party being thrown for the rest of the crews and the lower-ranking scientists. It'll probably be a lot more fun, and it's a good place to pick up rumors."

"Fine," said the skipper. "They'll probably learn a lot more than we will."

"Do you think those Satsuma people will give them any trouble?" asked Michelle.

"B'Shant's going with them," answered Finn.

"No trouble, then," said the skipper.

"And here comes K'Stin," said Torwald, "the belle of the ball."

The Viver entered. He wore a weapon harness studded with medallions and awards and hung with a variety of daggers and swords. He had painted himself from head to foot with stripes of red and green.

"Why the stripes, K'Stin?" asked Ham.

"The colors of the glorious Clan T'Chak. One must honor the Clan, even among inferior beings."

"You'll be the envy of everybody there," said Torwald.

"I know," said K'Stin complacently. "Yet do not feel too humiliated, for comparing the beauty of a Viver with that of you soft persons is as absurd as comparing the brilliance of a star with that of a luminous fungus." Kiril worked hard to keep a straight face. The Viver was almost supernaturally ugly, and the paint only increased the effect. But then, she reflected, the Vivers had their own standards of beauty, and they were far better equipped to enforce their opinions than were standard humans.

When Homer arrived, they left the ship. They found a somewhat smaller honor guard waiting for them. This guard was led by an officer older than the first, whose manner was far more congenial. It was plain that Pierce the diplomat was making a few adjustments.

The reception was being held in a vast room fitted with a lavish buffet and bar. All around the floor low-ranking servicemen were dancing attendance on the guests. Conversation stopped and all eyes turned their way when the doorkeeper announced the arrival of the personnel of the *Space Angel*. They were, indeed, celebrities. Pierce immediately rushed to greet them, and he steered Ham and the skipper off on a round of introductions, leaving the others to fend for themselves. They headed for the bar first. Torwald and Finn ordered drinks for their ladies.

"Would you like anything?" asked Lafayette.

"No, thanks," said Kiril. She knew that alcohol clouded one's judgment and slowed one's reflexes. In her experience, people with such afflictions ended up dead. Kiril had an almost Viverlike aversion to being dead. Lafayette signaled for the bartender.

"Have anything without alcohol?"

The bartender eyed Lafayette's nonmilitary dress with some disdain. "Admiral says no dope allowed on this voyage."

"That's not what I asked," Lafayette said, his face and neck going red. "The lady would like something nonalcoholic."

"Well, I'll see what I've got," said the bartender, looking about with insolent slowness.

Kiril had been studying the man's eyes closely. Now she leaned across the bar and said sweetly: "Hey, sailor, how would you like it if I told your commander what you've been smoking lately?" The bartender stared at her wide-eyed, swallowed hard, and quickly poured a glass full of something that was most definitely nonalcoholic.

Lafayette chuckled as they walked away. "Good stunt, Kiril." They found Torwald and Michelle, and Lafayette told them of their run in with the bartender.

"Bad blood already," said Torwald. "Well it's not surprising, with one tiny merchant crew in the middle of a big navy and line expedition."

"If that man's on drugs," Michelle said, "it means the med officer in charge of his section is taking bribes."

"That information is worth something," Torwald said.

"Navy standards must've fallen off since we were in," said Michelle. "Kiril, how did you know what that man was taking?"

"Anybody could see he was on Hyper," she said. "It's in the eyes."

"I couldn't see it," Michelle said, "and I'm a doctor."

They were interrupted by an officious junior diplomat who was bustling about, trying to introduce everybody to everybody else. "And you people are from the *Space Angel*, aren't you?" he said. "Have you met the head of the civilian mission?" He stepped aside to bring forward a very tall man who was accompanied by a shorter companion. "May I present Director Ramon Izquierda, of the Satsuma Line, and his nephew, Tomas Huerta."

Kiril held her breath, awaiting her friends' reaction. To her relief, they stayed formally correct, giving dignified nods and bows, accompanied by polite muttered nothings. She noticed that no handshakes were offered. Izquierda topped the tall Torwald and Finn by the better part of a foot. He was rail thin and his face was angular and aquiline, with a high forehead topped by a great mane of wavy gray hair. A generous mustache softened the harsh thinness of his mouth.

Huerta was a foot shorter, and a younger version of his uncle. Except for lacking the commanding height, he had to be a near double for the older man thirty years ago. It seemed the facial genes ran strong in the family. Kiril noticed that his eyes lit upon her with more than passing interest.

"So, you were among the personnel on the famous *Space Angel* expedition of a while back? Doubtless we would have met earlier, but I was away on an expedition when you returned." Izquierda's tones were suave and polished. "I just met your alien friend, a most remarkable creature. What a pity, though, that he must be a poet. A scientist would have been of far greater use to humanity."

"I think Homer knows far more of scientific matters than he lets on," said Torwald. "Possibly it's for the benefit of humanity that he keeps quiet about it."

Kiril felt it was safe to relax now, since the conversation was being confined to small talk. She was a bit disappointed in Izquierda. He was a formidable person, but she had been expecting something with horns and tail, from the way her shipmates had spoken about him. Then she heard the skipper's voice from behind her.

"Hello, Ramon. It's been a while." Izquierda's gaze passed over Kiril's head, and her spine went rigid. Her assessment of him underwent a radical reevaluation. Compared to this man, Pao Lin was a saint. Unconsciously she squeezed Lafayette's arm tightly, and he looked at her in amazement.

"Indeed it has been, Gertrude," said Izquierda, his tone still even and mellifluous. He nodded towards Ham. "I see that

Hamilton is still with you. Who would have thought that peacetime would bring us together again on an expedition?''

"Good question," said the skipper. "You've come up in the world since I saw you last."

"Rather the opposite seems true of you. Although I am sure that the independent merchant service has its attractions."

"At least I can be among friends," said the skipper. "That's something you can't enjoy on a board of directors."

"Alas, how true. However, power brings its own comforts."

The man from the diplomatic section was growing more alarmed by the second, but the conversation was interrupted by the approach of K'Stin. "Lord!" muttered Huerta under his breath. "What a hideous creature!" Kiril winced. The man wouldn't have dared such a remark had he realized the unbelievable sensitivity of a Viver's hearing. K'Stin, however, showed no sign that he had heard.

"Greetings, squishy ones," he began. "You see before you K'Stin, Free Guardian of the glorious Clan T'Chak."

"Greetings," said Izquierda. "My, Gertrude, you certainly have a . . . singular sort of crew. The true definition of the word 'motley' never struck me until now. I suppose K'Stin, here, would be handy to have along if you decided to take up piracy. I hear that the Vivers are great fighters."

The skipper flushed at the insult, but K'Stin went on, seemingly oblivious. "Very true. We are the greatest warriors in known space, and we despise only one thing more than a poor fighter or survivor."

"And what might that be?" asked Izquierda condescendingly.

"A coward," proclaimed K'Stin. "Especially one who traitorously abandons his own people to their death."

Izquierda went deathly white. Kiril had never seen such intense desire to murder in a man's eyes. "Do you know to whom you speak?" Each word was pronounced separately in a hissing whisper. Huerta looked at the Viver in horror.

K'Stin's chitinous lips bent almost into a grin, revealing the multiple rows of sawtoothed plates that served him for teeth. "Does this one wish to threaten me?" he said in his normal, noncommittal tone of voice. All of the *Angel*'s personnel leaped backwards, hauling Kiril with them, to be out of range of the Viver's murderous sword. A Viver had only one method of dealing with a threat. They did not believe in leaving live enemies behind their backs.

"Easy, K'Stin," said the skipper. "It's a mistake." She turned to Izquierda. "Ramon, don't misunderstand. He doesn't know you. Until he joined us, he'd never been off his Clan ship before."

After a tense moment Izquierda regained his color. "I see. K'Stin, I misunderstood. I mean no threat to you." K'Stin regarded him for a moment with the awful grin, then turned and walked away. Kiril watched him go. Had he meant to insult Izquierda? Despite the skipper's words, Kiril remembered that K'Stin had been present when the skipper had told her about Izquierda. And K'Stin must have heard Huerta's whispered comment.

Pierce came rushing up, worry in his face. "Is anything the matter? We had not wanted to bring your party and Director Izquierda's together in view of your old antipathy." He shot his subordinate a look that promised a royal dressing down. "But," he continued, "let's forget any unpleasantness for the moment. The banquet is about to begin. Please come this way." They trailed off after Pierce into the next room.

"I can't say Izquierda's my favorite sort of person," Lafayette said, "but I'm a little disappointed. I was expecting a man-eating ogre at least."

"Are you crazy?" exclaimed Kiril. "That man's the most vicious killer I've ever seen in my life! He had me fooled too, at first, but when he looked at the skipper, I saw through him. Believe me, I know that breed when I see it."

"Well, if this is your normal reaction, I hope we run into a few more nasty characters." For the first time she noticed she was still clutching Lafayette's arm. She was surprised that it felt so natural. Back in Civis Astra any girl who lived without protection had to provide her own. That meant keeping all men at arm's length or better.

"Well," she said, "first time for everything."

They were led into a chamber as vast as the reception room, its walls hung with priceless Taurus IV tapestries and lined with parallel rows of tables. One long table was at right angles to the rest and stood on a slightly raised dais at one end of the room. Grand Admiral Nagamitsu was already seated at this table along with a few other brass-heavy officers and some members of the diplomatic and scientific missions. Izquierda and Huerta were also seated there. The *Angel*'s crew were conducted to their seats at the lower tables. When a waiter tried to seat the skipper and the mate at a lower table, they brushed past him and went to the higher one.

"Um, Captain HaLevy," said Pierce, "this table is reserved for naval officers of commodore standing and above, line officers of comparable rank, senior diplomats, and guests of the scientific mission. I'm afraid . . ." He spread his hands helplessly. Kiril watched the little power play with interest. She caught the glare of triumph that Izquierda shot towards the skipper.

"I beg to differ, your Excellency," said the skipper. "According to the regs, any retired or reserve officer, at any formal function, is entitled to the privileges pertaining to the highest rank that officer held *even temporarily* during active service. If you'll check my records, you'll note that at the time of the Li Po invasion, I held the brevet rank of commodore for six weeks. It's all here." She unclasped her spacer's bracelet and tossed it on the table in front of Pierce. "My second officer, that time as now, Hamilton Sylvester, here"—Ham took a bow—"is my escort. I demand to be seated with the perquisites of my rank."

Pierce looked around for help. This was a situation even he had never run up against.

"She's quite right," said Nagamitsu. His tone was emotionless but his eyes held a faint twinkle. Ham and the skipper were seated, causing some changes of arrangement. Last of all Homer was ensconced on a specially-made platform.

"What does your friend drink?" asked Pierce in a whisper. "I fear I've forgotten to find out." He was obviously embarrassed.

"I guess you can't think of everything," said Ham. "Ol' Homer's fond of turpentine, with a little prussic acid. He can eat just about anything."

"Check quartermaster stores for some turpentine," said

Nagamitsu, without batting an eyelash. "And the labs should have some prussic acid." The nearest waiter darted away, and Nagamitsu turned to the skipper, grinning. "When a navy vessel runs out of turpentine, she shouldn't be allowed to space."

Kiril turned her attention from the high table to her own. She was acutely conscious of the beauty of many of the women surrounding her. Many of them were navy officers, some were from the lines. She wondered if they were all born that way or could they just afford high-class surgery? It struck her that she did not come off all that unfavorably by comparison.

The waiters began bringing in the first courses. Most of the food was Earth-raised and she was unfamiliar with it, as she was with most food. What she lacked in experience, though, she made up for with enthusiasm. After the chilled vichyssoise, the waiter set a lobster before her. She looked at it with dismay.

"Hey, Lafayette," she said, "eating this'd be kind of like chewing on old Homer. I'd feel like a cannibal."

"Homer's not a real crustacean," Lafayette assured her. "He just looks like one. That lobster's more closely related to you than it is to Homer." Kiril had her doubts, but the smell of the lobster and the butter sauce overcame them. Lafayette showed her how to tackle the thing. She caught on quickly and ate two.

"Take it easy," said Lafayette as waiters passed carrying platters heaped with entrees. "Just pick small amounts of everything. Those two steaks look a little excessive."

"How come?" Kiril asked. "That's what this is all about, isn't it? Eating?"

"Sure, but there are conventions to follow. Most people here don't have as many lean years to make up for as you."

"Well, let them spend a few years fighting sewer lizards for scraps and I'll let them dictate how I eat." Despite her defiance, Kiril watched the others more closely and tried to eat, like them, with more circumspection. It took an effort of will.

"Excuse me," said a gilded lady across the table from Kiril. "You're with the *Space Angel*'s company, aren't you?"

"That's right," Kiril said, working on a helping of Peking duck.

"Were you on the expedition that reached the Core Star? I

don't recall seeing your features on the news at the time."

"No," said Kiril, reaching for some curried lamb. "I've signed on since then."

"Ah, what a pity," the woman said. "But you must have heard all about it from the rest of the crew, and from that marvelous little alien. Tell me, is it true that he's the most erudite creature in existence? It's hard to believe that anything so—so—peculiar-looking, is a poet and a scholar."

"I've been working with Homer lately," Kiril said.

"Oh, really? On what, poetry?"

"No, he's been doing a study on human profanity. Do you know the Taurus IV word for—"

"Ah, yes, wonderful being, Homer," said Lafayette, breaking in abruptly. "He's a little disconcerting at first, but you get used to him." He helped Kiril to a load of Yorkshire pudding, perhaps in hopes of shutting her up. A welcome distraction was provided by K'Stin, who was regaling his neighbors down the table with tales of his bloodthirsty exploits.

"And then, at the great Post-Adolescent Talent Contest, I fought the mighty B'Kin," he said with enthusiasm. "I ripped off his pectoral chitin and disemboweled—"

"But, ah, Mr. K'Stin," said a junior diplomat, looking rather green, "doesn't it damage your people's renowned posture of defense for your young warriors to be killing each other?"

"Hah, it takes more than a little disemboweling to kill a Viver," K'Stin asserted. "Once, at the Inter-Clan Fun Fair, the estimable K'Tok and I fought with heavy billhooks and he beheaded me." He thumped the thick stalk of interlocking rings that served him for a neck. "Grew back together good as new." It might have been true. Nobody knew for sure what it took to kill a Viver since nobody had accomplished the feat.

The rest of the dinner was occupied with small talk. Kiril noticed that people avoided talking about the mission. She got the distinct impression that they didn't know what the mission was all about anyway. She asked Lafayette about this as people began leaving the table. "It's likely," he said. "The navy people can be sent anywhere, they don't have to be told why. As for the scientific and diplomatic people . . ." He shrugged. "I don't know. We do know that we weren't told not to talk about it. Maybe everybody's just playing cagey. I have a feeling that there's a lot of politics being played here. Now, look, we're expected to socialize for a while. That means I can't monopolize you. Circulate, make small talk, but avoid prying questions. If somebody starts to talk about something you don't want to bring up, or it's something you don't know anything about, just change the subject. It's expected.''

"I can take care of myself," she said. Actually, she wasn't so sure. This wasn't the streets. She went ahead and took the plunge, keeping her shipmates' locations in mind in case she should feel the need of backup. She found her task to be fairly easy. Everybody wanted to talk a great deal and say very little. It was almost fun.

"We haven't properly met," said a voice. Kiril turned and her heart lurched. For a split second she thought she was facing Izquierda, then realized that she wasn't looking high enough and this man had black hair. It was Huerta.

"I guess not," she said, covering her confusion. "I'm Kiril. I just joined the *Angel* a few weeks ago." She spoke slowly, trying to keep her grammar straight.

"I wanted to say I'm sorry about that little scene a while ago. I know my uncle and your captain have some kind of feud dating back to the War. It's a shame that they should hold a grudge so long."

"I'll go along with you there," she said. That seemed safe enough. Her guard was up, but he didn't seem to be nearly as menacing as his uncle.

"Well, I just wanted you to know that, whatever his grudge is, I don't share it. I certainly wouldn't extend it to the rest of you, in any case. This is going to be a long expedition, and I hope we can be friends."

"That sounds good to me," Kiril said. She wondered whether he meant all of them or herself in particular. She hoped not. The last thing she wanted was to start liking this handsome *schlucter*. "Let's just figure the truce has been signed and we're back to square one, okay?"

"That will have to do," he said, smiling, "at least for a start." He had one of the better smiles she'd encountered. Then she reminded herself that she didn't trust smiles. He glanced over her shoulder. "Ah, here comes the director to collect me. It seems I must go." He gave her a courtly bow and actually took her hand and kissed it. It didn't even occur to her to whip out a knife. "I hope we'll be seeing a lot of each other."

She watched his retreating, caped back. Down, girl, she thought. This is the last thing you need.

4

"Hey, Tor, what do you know about court-martials?" Kiril and Torwald were walking aft through the hold towards the engine room. Michelle had decided that, since the thrusters were idle during their long haul to the edge of the system in the hold of the TFCS, Kiril could now go back and learn something of the engineering section.

"The correct plural is 'courts-martial,'" said Torwald.

"Don't be a pain. Come on, how do they work?"

"Why the sudden interest?"

"It's that *schturtzl* Izquierda. He's probably got it in for us, right? And it's because of this military trial, right? So I'd like to find out as much about this mess as I can. After all, my neck's on the block, too."

"All right," said Torwald with exaggerated patience, "just to set your mind at ease. A general court martial, the kind that tried Izquierda, is a board consisting of a varying number of officers, depending on what's available under wartime conditions. There's no jury. The senior officer is president of the court. There's a prosecutor, usually an officer from the JAG corps.''

"JAG?''

"Judge Advocate General. And there's a defense attorney. In an emergency, though, any officer can be appointed to defend or prosecute. When the arguments are over, the board votes guilty or not guilty. Majority decides. In case of a tie, the president casts the deciding vote. They can drag on for weeks, but I've sat on courts held during battles and sieges that lasted a few minutes. A general court can order any punishment, including execution.''

"If that court found Izquierda guilty of what he did, why didn't they just stand him up against a wall and shoot him?''

"They should have. However, if conditions permit, they have to allow the defendant time to appeal to a higher court. Izquierda appealed all the way to the Council and got off. I didn't hear about the incident or the trial until after the War, like most people. By the time Izquierda got his appeal through, people were sick of the War and just wanted to put it behind them. He must have counted on that.''

They came to a big hatch marked Engine Room. Torwald stuck his head inside and called out: "Ahoy, the black gang.'' Kiril shook her head. Spacers were full of archaic forms and usages. It seemed silly to hear that someone on a fairly modern space ship should have to hail the engine crew with a phrase from the ancient, coal-driven ocean vessels. They were a proud and touchy lot, though, so she kept her opinions to herself.

Inside, she looked about with interest. The bulkheads, where they were not covered with readout plates, were white and immaculate. Towards the stern two pits housed the thrusters employed to get the ship clear of the solar system. Slung between them was a huge cone, its apex pointed towards the nose of the ship. Its tip was transparent, and inside she could see suspended a metallic mobius band.

"What's that?'' she asked, pointing toward the cone.

"That's the Whooppee drive generator,'' said Achmed. The Arab sat next to Lafayette on a bench below a worktable. The two had disassembled an esoteric piece of apparatus and were cleaning it with tiny sonic disrupters. "This is the Fuel Flow Regulator, Kiril,'' Achmed continued. "It controls the flow of nuclear fuel to the two thrusters and makes sure they stay in balance.'' He pointed out the various parts of the instrument, and Kiril soaked it all up, fascinated. Torwald sat down and picked up a brush and a bottle of solvent and began helping the engineers. Work and instruction went on for an hour. Achmed did most of the talking. Lafayette seemed sullen, for some reason. She suspected that he had seen Huerta kissing her hand the night before. Well, what business was it of his, anyway?

Achmed called a halt, and the three men drew cups of the inevitable, horrid coffee from a wall dispenser.

''How could we find out about Izquierda's trial?'' Kiril asked, doggedly sticking to her earlier train of thought. Achmed and Lafayette stared at her in puzzlement, then looked at Torwald for elucidation.

''She started in a while back on courts-martial and Izquierda's case. She wants to know all about it. Thinks it's important.''

''She could be right,'' said Achmed. He turned to Kiril again. ''Do you want to know how the trial went?''

''Of course not,'' Kiril said impatiently. How could these people be so dense? ''We know how the trial went. What I want to know is what happened to the board members since the trial. And what about the witnesses who testified against Izquierda? Don't you people have any sense of self-preservation at all?''

''I think she's got something,'' said Lafayette reluctantly. ''Where can we find that information?''

''The full Archives of the Confederation are contained in the computer banks of every capital ship of the navy,'' said Achmed.

''That's the place to look, then,'' said Kiril.

''You don't just walk into the computer room of a navy ship and sit down at the console,'' Lafayette said. ''They're loaded with classified information.''

''It's out of the question,'' added Torwald. ''They'd never let one of us close to that computer. Even if they did, Izquierda's people would get wind of it and see what we were inquiring about. No, it's a good idea, but it won't work.''

''I'll bet they'd let Homer in,'' she said sweetly. She took deep satisfaction in the way they looked at her with new respect.

* * *

The crew, grouped around the mess table, waited for Homer to begin. Kiril smiled smugly as she sat next to Homer, taking a quiet satisfaction in her coup. Even the skipper had to admit that Kiril had spotted a possibility they had all missed. Homer made a throat-clearing sound. He didn't need to, since he had no throat to clear. He knew, however, that humans were more comfortable, for some reason, if these sounds were made prior to a lengthy speech.

"I was granted access to the computer," he began, "on the pretext that I was studying some seventeenth-century commentaries written in Flemish on Dante. Of course, I actually *was* making such inquiries, I simply did not explain what other studies I was making."

"Sure, Homer," said the skipper. "Now, what did you find about the court-martial board?"

"There were nine officers on the board," said Homer. "Of these, four later died in action during the Confed-Trium War. Their names were—"

"Forget 'em," said Ham. "Those were probably legitimate deaths in action, and if they weren't, we'd have a time proving it. What about the others?"

"President of the court was Rear Admiral Chi'Ching Fu. He retired after the War and lived on a small space yacht. It was lost on a routine trip from Earth to Luna. Of the other four, Rear Admiral Ian Donleavy, on Reserve status, was testing a new impulse engine for the Navy Mark Thirty-five Moray when the engine detonated. Cause of detonation was never determined."

"Bar Kochba, Inc. made that ship," said the skipper. "They're a good firm."

"Who made those experimental engines?" asked Bert.

"Reith Power Systems," said Homer.

"A wholly-owned subsidiary of Satsuma-MacKintosh Heavy Industries," added Ham.

"And the rest?" asked Michelle.

"Captain Richard Probert left the service after the War and founded Probert Aerospace Service, a small freighting line. It ran into peculiar difficulties from the start: ships pirated, asteroid collisions, disappearances, and the like. Captain Probert eventually committed suicide.

"Captain Suleiman Ramjan and Commander Sebastien

Romero Ortega, both on the board of the court-martial, went into partnership after the War, forming a company to exploit the mineral wealth of Senmut, a planet both had served on during the War. There was friction between the two, and one morning both were found dead in a park near one of their factories. The finding of the investigative committee was death mutually inflicted in an unauthorized duel.''

"That takes care of the court," said Torwald. The rest had grown more quiet with each recitation of misadventure.

"What about the witnesses?" asked Kiril.

"To make the story brief," said Homer, "in all, some forty witnesses were called to testify, after the original denunciation by then-Captain Gertrude HaLevy. Of these, twenty-seven died later in the War, most in the Li Po action. Of the thirteen others, two died of natural causes and the rest in circumstances of violence or misadventure never subsequently solved by police."

"Except for one," said Ham.

"Precisely," said Homer. "The sole survivor of that court is one Gertrude HaLevy, now Skipper of *Space Angel*."

"What about the prosecutor?" asked Lafayette.

"Captain Dingaan AmaZulu died of an unknown virus on Cetewayo shortly after the War. It was a lingering and extremely painful death."

"And the defense attorney?" asked the skipper. "I've forgotten his name."

"Mr. Wesley Stoddard was a civilian attorney when hired to represent Commodore Izquierda. The case was lost, but Mr. Stoddard was successful on appeal. He is now a director of the Satsuma Line, and head of the legal department."

"Nice to know somebody came out of this alive and successful," said the skipper. The quip rang hollow. They were thinking the same thing; Fifty-two people involved with that court, of those, all dead but two, one of them a director of Satsuma, the other the skipper of *Space Angel*.

"So what's our next move?" asked Ham.

"Simple," said K'Stin. "Kill Izquierda." The Viver's suggestion was eminently predictable.

"There are laws against personal vengeance, K'Stin," said the skipper, "and it didn't escape me that you tried to set him up at the banquet."

"It is your life," K'Stin said. "He will try to kill you sooner or later, and that endangers us all."

"K'Stin's right about that part of it," Torwald said. "Murder is out, but so is suicide. We can't take any chances. We're not dealing with an ordinary criminal; this man is almost supernatural."

"We have a great deal of damning information here," Michelle said. "We have officials of the government and the military right here on this expedition. Why don't we take this to them and expose him?"

"Expose what?" asked Bert. "We have no proof that he engineered all those deaths. Most of those involved were spacers in high-risk fields. It's not inconceivable that they all could die in the space of a few years. Unlikely, certainly, but not beyond the bounds of reason. We'll need more evidence than this to denounce him."

"What's it matter?" Kiril said. "We already know that this man committed one of the biggest atrocities of the War and got off with a kiss on the cheek. And he's *lots* richer and more powerful and influential than he was back then. You think he's gonna do a day of hard time just for knocking off seventeen or eighteen people? Forget it. Your Confed government is just Civis Astra on a big scale, and he's the biggest K'ang leader around."

"I'm afraid you're right," said the skipper. "It's going to come down to him or me, and right now we have to let him make the next move. I wish I knew why he saved me for last."

"And why he picked this mission to carry out whatever he has in mind," added Torwald.

The planet, now designated Eingma, floated above their heads in the observation bubble. This was the compartment opening off Finn's navigation chamber, where Kiril had seen Nancy playing her instrument. It was rarely used, since navigators these days never bothered with eyeball sighting for their calculations, and the instruments had long since been ripped out, but it was the only place on the ship from which the outside could be seen.

There wasn't much to see. The visible hemisphere was

mostly under cloud cover, drifting across the oceans and continents in long streaks. Low in the southern hemisphere, the whorl of a small hurricane was taking shape.

"Doesn't look like much," said Kiril, slightly disappointed.

"You'd be surprised," said Torwald. "The planets that look the most spectacular from space are the ones we can't live on. If they have a cotton-ball look, like this one, it means there's free water, and that's the biggest single factor in making a planet desirable for colonization."

"But somebody else was here first, this time," Kiril pointed out.

"All too true," said the skipper. "We can only guess why, but I'm willing to guess if nobody else is. My guess is, they're oxygen breathers and their life system requires liquid water, just like us."

"Why's that?" Kiril asked.

"Because we're always on the lookout for planets just like this one. In fact, we almost never set up housekeeping on any other kind unless it has something really valuable that we want. Why knock yourself out taming a hostile environment when there's planets like this where you can move right in without a lot of terraforming and atmosphere suits?"

"Makes sense," Kiril said. She could just make out the shapes of the two tremendous ships in the far distance. They had left the hold of the TFCS as soon as they had reached this system. It made them feel safer, for no particular reason.

"When does the fun begin?" asked Finn.

"We're supposed to wait for orders to land," the skipper said. "The navy's tried to establish communication, but so far no answer on any frequency. That's not surprising. Then they send in a scoutship to check for hostility. If it's all clear, the civilian party and higher-up navy people will go down in a shuttle from the Supernova. Eventually, maybe they'll remember us and invite us down."

"Are the navy ship and the Supernova going to land?" Kiril asked.

"Neither of those monsters is designed to land," Torwald said. "They'll stay in orbit and try to look impressive."

"Any signs of alien activity so far?" Michelle asked.

"None we've detected or been informed of," said the skipper. "Come on, let's go back to the bridge and see what the screens tell us."

The main screen showed the alien base much as they had seen it before, hazed as if by intervening atmosphere. No magnification gave them any clearer idea of what they were looking at. A brilliant point of light appeared, descending toward a dark, blank area near the buildings.

"That's the navy probe going in," said Torwald. "We should be getting word before long."

They heard sooner than expected. Less than eight hours after the navy probe had landed, the *Space Angel* was notified to stand by for landing.

They waited in the cargo bay as the ramp lowered. The *Space Angel* stood on her landing shock absorbers in the shadow of the Supernova's shuttle. Ten ships the size of the *Angel* could have stood on the shadow. The wide expanse of the alien landing field was deserted except for a party of the human mission gathered around the base of the huge shuttle.

"Why didn't they just bring us down in that thing?" Torwald said. "If they want to impress these aliens, you'd think they'd want to keep the poor old *Angel* out of sight."

"We'll probably find out all too soon," said the skipper. "If Izquierda's behind it, and he most likely is, then we won't like the reason. No sense stalling. Let's go join them."

They descended the ramp, their eyes nervously scanning about, but there was no movement from the distant structures. They had been ordered to carry no weapons, for fear of provoking an incident with the aliens, if and when they should arrive. It did give them some comfort to have the Vivers along. When they reached the Supernova's shuttle, an officer passed them through the cordon of Spacer Marines that surrounded the party, their beam rifles at port arms.

"How come these jarheads can carry guns when nobody else can?" Kiril asked.

"They won't fire except on the admiral's orders," said Torwald. "There isn't a man among 'em who doesn't have ten years of psychdiscipline behind him."

"Quiet, you two," said the skipper. "I do all the talking until we know where we stand." They went to the knot of people surrounding Nagamitsu. All the navy and line officers were in full dress uniform. Nagamitsu's outfit was identical to that of his fellow officers except for his collar insignia and a long, two-handed Japanese sword thrust edge-upward through his sash. Its handle was braided with black silk tape. He was flanked by Pierce and Izquierda.

"Nothing so far, Captain HaLevy," said Nagamitsu. "If there were going to be hostile action, it probably would have happened by now. We'd like your personnel to be here when they make their move. Especially Homer."

"Homer," said the skipper, "front and center. Admiral, what do you want the rest of us to do . . ." She trailed off as Nagamitsu's face took on a distant look, as if he were listening to some faraway voice. "Alien vessel coming in for a landing," he said.

"How's he know that?" Kiril asked Nancy in a whisper.

"Receiver implanted behind his ear," Nancy said absently, her eyes scanning overhead. Kiril looked up, too. The air was suddenly crackling with tension.

"Damn!" Torwald said. "I thought they'd send out a party from the base. This is inconsiderate, if you ask me."

"Nobody asked you, Tor," the skipper said. "Now pipe down."

Now they could see it; a black network of spheres and struts, globular instead of circular like the one in Ng's holos. It was plummeting like a stone. "Something's wrong," muttered Nagamitsu. "She's out of control." They braced themselves for the shock with gritted teeth. The more experienced threw themselves to the ground and covered their heads. Alarm sirens began shrieking from the shuttle.

Abruptly, twenty meters above the pad, the ship halted. There was no deceleration. One instant the ship was dropping in an uncontrolled fall, the next it was at rest. The ground party began picking themselves up and dusting off their clothes.

"What's holding it up?" asked someone.

"Flying carpets, for all I know," said the skipper. "But if they wanted to impress us, they sure accomplished it."

"Splendid beginning for negotiations," said Izquierda, a faint, sardonic smile on his lips. He had remained standing throughout the incident and his uniform was immaculate.

"We don't know yet that there's anything to be negotiated," the skipper pointed out. "They may not even be interested in us." Three hundred meters away the fantastic vessel settled to the pad.

"Something will have to be agreed upon," Izquierda said. "Our two species have now impinged upon each other's space. This is only the first encounter. There will be many more. Interested or not, they have to establish whether relations between us are to be friendly or hostile."

"I'm here to offer them a lasting peace," said Nagamitsu. "We'll deal from the best position of strength we can, but we can't risk precipitating conflict. Humanity simply can't afford another war at this time."

"Amen to that," said Pierce, resplendent in striped trousers, swallowtail coat, and topper.

"Peace for now, perhaps," Izquierda said. "But if they're an expanding race, as we are, we'll come into conflict sooner or later."

"No need to borrow trouble, Director," said Pierce. "However, friendly or hostile, we would do well to learn as much of them as we can."

"I still don't see how that thing hangs together," Torwald said. By unspoken consent, the *Space Angel*'s crew had drawn a few paces away from the brass. "It doesn't look like structural metal. No welds or rivets that I can make out, and everything's so irregular. Maybe it's some kind of plastic or synthetic." He took out a folding viewer from a tunic pocket and scanned the alien ship. After a minute he refolded the viewer and put it back in his pocket. "No good. That masking works even this close."

"We'll just have to wait until they trust us enough to give us a close look," Ham said.

"Something's happening," the skipper said. "It's opening up."

A split had opened in one of the larger spheres, widening toward the bottom. The babble of conversation hushed, and people began to arrange themselves in some kind of order, with Nagamitsu and Pierce to the fore. The marines continued to stand in their protective circle, as they would until ordered to do otherwise or death overtook them.

The first of the aliens appeared at the top of a tonguelike ramp that extruded from the alien ship to touch the landing pad. Distance was too great to make out detail, but it was erect, two-legged, and approximately human-sized. More moved in behind it as it walked down the ramp. There were at least twenty by the time the ramp pulled back into the ship and the split closed.

About halfway between ship and shuttle, the aliens walked out of their ship's masking field. It was a startling effect, as if someone fiddling with sighting controls had all at once hit the right combination and the subject suddenly jumped into sharp focus.

The aliens were not human, but neither were they so different that it was difficult to think of them as a spacegoing species. Their walk was not quite that of humans, although it was difficult to place just where the difference lay. They had knees and elbows in roughly the same places as humans. Their skin was blue, and they had a lot of it showing. Except for boots and close-fitting helmetlike caps, they wore only a harness of straps to support tools and small pouches. Nothing showed externally to determine gender. They had short, vestigial tails which twitched continually.

Their faces had a basic similarity to the human norm; two eyes, two nostrils, one mouth. The mouth had no lips, and the nose was a perfunctory, slightly raised bar of flesh. The eyes were rectangles with rounded corners, above boldly protruding cheekbones. The eyeballs were slate gray, with horizontal, slit pupils running almost the entire width of the ball.

Plainly, these creatures could not share the accepted body language of humans, but some things seemed to be the common property of upright, bipedal life forms. These aliens seemed to be cautious and wary, but their every move radiated confidence to the border of arrogance.

Nagamitsu noted the dangling straps and clips on the harnesses of the approaching aliens. "They've disarmed to meet us."

"Not all of them," said Izquierda. "The one in the lead had a long, daggerlike weapon in his waist belt."

"Neither did I," said Nagamitsu, touching the long sword in his sash. "They wear obsolete weapons for ceremonial purposes. That gives us some common grounds." He turned to the sergeant of the guard. "Sergeant, give us an open crescent and present arms."

"Aye aye, sir!" The sergeant turned to his men and spoke softly into his throat mike. The circle opened as two wings split and the men trotted smoothly into crescent formation with the open side toward the aliens. They snapped to present arms and held the pose effortlessly. The alien in the lead raised a six-fingered hand and made a waving motion, taking in all of the marines.

"I think he just returned the salute," Torwald said. "This doesn't look so good."

"At least we have some basis for communication," Michelle said. "I was afraid they'd be so alien it'd take us years just to figure out how to say hello."

"Yeah," Torwald said, "but everything about these people says military."

"They are a fighting species," said K'Stin. "The Clan and the Folk must hear of this."

"Sshh," hissed the skipper. "Let's hear what's going on."

Pierce stepped forward and strode to within three paces of the alien. He bowed stiffly and said: "I bring greetings from the Confederated Planets, and their wishes for a long, prosperous, peaceful, and mutually beneficial relationship." He smiled and waited. He was an experienced diplomat and was prepared to hold the smile indefinitely.

The lead alien began to speak. At least, its lips moved. From time to time they would hear a sound, but mostly there was silence. Whatever the alien had to say, it was brief. Its lips stopped moving and the sounds ceased.

"Homer," said Nagamitsu, "they're all yours." The little crustacean stepped forward and launched into his repertoire of languages. This occupied some time, since Homer knew many hundreds of tongues. As the minutes dragged on, Kiril began to fidget.

"This is going to take a while, Kiril," said the skipper. She lit up a stogie. "No need for you to stand around here doing nothing. Why don't you wander around? Nobody'd notice you, and you might hear something interesting. Like over there where Izquierda and the admiral and those other high-rankers are."

"Right," said Kiril, glad to have something to do. This was something she was experienced at. She had cultivated eavesdropping early in life as a valuable skill. The knot of exalted personages had drawn together a little apart from the rest. Kiril wandered in their direction. As the skipper had predicted, none of them paid her the slightest attention.

Izquierda was saying, "We have here a clear and present danger to humanity. That vessel"—he pointed to the fantastic alien ship—"is a violation of every known law of physics. Who knows what other powers these aliens control? I counsel that we take the utmost precautions to prevent a sneak attack on ourselves and to safeguard the locations of all human-occupied worlds and installations." Kiril could recognize the sound of a man playing to an audience, and she could see that the words were having the desired effect. The look among the gathered notables was one of agreement. For some reason, Izquierda wanted to be on record as saying these things. Recording instruments were picking up every detail of the historic occasion.

"It shouldn't be necessary to point out, Director," said Nagamitsu, "that you are not here for the purpose of counsel. I have taken every precaution necessary to protect this expedition. Believe me, they are considerable. As for the protection of human space, that is provided for under old regulations, as you perfectly well know. The records will self-destruct unless approached with proper coding. Even so, I've had the fail-safe systems checked and rechecked."

"Even on that ship?" said Izquierda, pointing at the *Space Angel*.

"Captain HaLevy has surrendered all tapes, chips, charts, and other materials pertaining to the locations of human systems. They'll be destroyed along with the rest, should it become necessary. Why all this concern, Director?"

"I'm a cautious man," Izquierda answered.

"That's what your record says," Nagamitsu said, his face expressionless. Izquierda glared at the admiral for a moment, then whirled and stalked off.

"Hello, there." There was a touch on Kiril's shoulder and she spun on her heel, hands automatically going for her daggers before she remembered that she had been forced to leave them aboard ship. It was Izquierda's nephew, Huerta.

"I didn't mean to startle you, please forgive me."

"It's all right," Kiril said, slightly flustered. "You just kind of sneaked up on me."

"I thought I was making sufficient noise," said Huerta with a faint smile. "Perhaps your attention was otherwise engaged."

"Uh, yeah, maybe so," she said lamely. "What do you think of them?" She gestured with her chin towards the aliens. She was less interested in his opinion than in changing the subject.

"I must agree with my uncle. I think the danger they represent far outweighs any cultural or scientific advantage we might gain from them."

"A lot of people seem to hold otherwise."

"True. Perhaps they're right. Let's hope so, in any case. Your friend over there doesn't seem to be having much success in communicating with them."

"He didn't think that he would. Homer told me he's spent most of his life near the center of the galaxy. The chances that a species out this far towards the rim would recognize a language he knows are millions to one, he said. But if they give him any kind of clue, he'll figure theirs out faster than a computer."

"A valuable creature to have along," said Huerta. He gave Homer a long, calculating look. They watched for a few minutes longer, until Homer's recitation ended.

"Any luck?" called Nagamitsu.

"None," Homer replied. "At least, they haven't responded to any speech I know."

"Between you and our computers, maybe we can figure something out," Nagamitsu said.

Izquierda had returned, his former anger completely gone or at least smothered. "Did anything in their attitude impress you as belligerent, Homer?" he asked.

"Nothing."

"I understand you're a peaceful creature, Homer," Izquierda said. "Perhaps you put too pacific an interpretation on things."

"Possibly," said Homer. "It is true that in all my life I've found few species as suicidally warlike as you humans while still being intelligent. Ordinarily, the two qualities do not appear together.''

"Belligerent or not," Nagamitsu said, "I'm betting that they'll play cautious. We're as much an unknown quantity to them as they are to us. They've seen that we have two different species on this mission. They have no way of knowing that we acquired Homer somewhat by accident. They may take the Vivers for a third species. For all they know, we represent some sort of multispecies alliance. Even the most warlike of beings wouldn't precipitate action against a foe of utterly unknown strength and capabilities.''

Pierce joined them. The aliens were now walking back towards their ship. "It looks as if proceedings are over for the day," said the diplomat. "Now we'll put our computers to work on our scant data, and I'll wager that they will be doing exactly the same thing.''

"All personnel," Nagamitsu announced, "prepare to up ship in one hour. We'll return tomorrow. Captain HaLevy, you'll return to orbit as well.''

"Why don't we just stick around, Admiral," Torwald said. "I'll bet Finn and I can entice them into a card game this evening. We've never failed before.''

"Captain HaLevy," Nagamitsu said patiently, "you and your talented crew will kindly up ship in one hour.''

"Aye aye, Admiral," she said.

Kiril was about to rejoin her shipmates when Huerta stopped her. "Miss, ah, Kiril, isn't it?''

"Just Kiril.''

"Well, Kiril, I have a confession to make: I'm bored to death with navy and line people. I've lived among them nearly every day of my life. I think this friction between us and the free freighters is stupid, as well as depriving me of interesting company. Would you like to come up as my guest and let me show you the Supernova? She's the pride of the line.''

The shutters immediately snapped shut behind Kiril's eyes as her mind worked furiously to analyze this new situation. What was he up to? "What about the others?" she said, gesturing towards the rest of the *Angel*'s crew.

"Oh, they're all old spacers. They know all about ships. You'd be much more fun to show off for, and I could pretend to be an expert.'' His smile was disarming, but no smile had ever disarmed Kiril. Still, it seemed to be worth a try, if only to find out what was behind all this. At least, she told herself, that was the reason.

''Do you think your uncle would go for it?''

''Probably not, but then, Uncle Ramon doesn't always approve of everything I do. He has more important things on his mind just now. I doubt he'd even notice. The Supernova's a passenger liner, you know. It's got scads of unused cabins just now. I'll put you up in one of the luxury suites overnight and you can rejoin your ship when we come down for the next round of talks in the morning.''

''This suite got a lock on the door?'' she asked suspiciously.

He laughed heartily. He had a nice laugh, she thought. ''You're a cautious one, aren't you? Yes, all our cabins are totally secure. Rich people always demand security.''

She faked a moment of thought, then: ''Sure, I'll come along. If I can convince my skipper. I'll go ask.''

Kiril reported briefly on what she had overheard on her eavesdropping assignment first. ''Izquierda tries to stir up trouble with every breath he takes,'' Torwald commented. ''How come?''

''Maybe it's just his nature,'' said the skipper. ''Come on, let's go back to the ship and get some chow before we up ship. Even in the midst of historical events, people gotta eat.''

Then Kiril told them about the invitation. The skipper favored her with the kind of look reserved for the dangerously demented. ''What?'' she shouted, then, in a less public tone: ''You accepted an invite from that human tick's nephew? Have you gone completely space happy?''

''Come on, Skipper,'' said Michelle, ''how do you know Huerta's anything like his uncle? I'd hate to be judged by the way some of my relatives behave.''

''Nor would I,'' Finn contributed. ''Why, some of my family stayed sober and respectable all their lives.''

''I don't like it, Skipper,'' Lafayette protested. ''We can't let a girl go over there alone with all those line people.'' He glared at Kiril and she glared back.

''Who made you my guardian?'' she demanded.

''Huerta's the director's nephew, you young idiot,'' said

Bert. "Nobody'd dare molest his guest, for fear of being sacked and beached for life."

"It's Huerta that worries me most," said Lafayette stubbornly.

"No worry," K'Stin rumbled. "Huerta touch this little one and she doesn't like it, he require surgery. She is tougher than him. Tougher than most of you." The Viver was a connoisseur of survival aptitude, so his opinion had to be taken seriously.

"I can take care of myself, all right," Kiril insisted. "I did pretty well the sixteen years of my life before you came along."

"And," said Torwald, "a spy in the enemy camp isn't a bad idea."

The skipper mulled it over for a minute. "All right," she said at last. "You can go. Keep your eyes and ears open, but don't go snooping on your own. Just smile, be nice, keep him at a distance, and whatever you do, don't attract Izquierda's attention. He kills people like disinfectant kills bacteria."

"I'll be okay," Kiril said. "See you tomorrow." She walked back to the huge shuttle, where Huerta stood waiting by the ramp. Most of the party had already boarded.

"That must have been quite a discussion," Huerta commented.

"They were telling me to mind my manners, but they agreed that they can get along without me for tonight. Let's go see your ship."

5

Kiril was glad that she had experienced the luxury of the diplomatic section of the TFCS, because it kept her from rubbernecking foolishly aboard the Supernova. The shuttle had been a strictly utilitarian vehicle, and the flight to orbit had been spent in nervous small talk with Huerta. They had stopped first at the TFCS to drop off navy personnel, then had proceeded to the Supernova, orbiting only a few kilometers away.

"Is all of it like this?" Kiril asked. They were in a huge reception area. A fountain arched its spray thirty feet overhead, and a divided staircase arched around the fountain to an upper level. High above the spray a crystal chandelier dangled from the ceiling.

Huerta laughed. "No. This is the entrance to the luxury accommodations. There are tourist and immigrant accommodations as well, and cargo space. Those areas are still largely under construction. We brought the work crews along on this voyage, at double pay. I understand my uncle and the other directors got into some heated arguments with the navy over that. The line insisted on keeping its construction schedule, and my uncle has to vouch for our security.''

"Is this the only Supernova?" she asked. She ran a hand along the smooth wood of the stair banister. It was rubbed to a beautiful gloss.

"It's the first, but soon we'll have an entire fleet. There are fifty more under construction, and more to follow. We'll sell off the old Class Ones to the smaller lines."

"Fifty. It's hard to believe." They ascended the stair. It was carpeted so thickly that her boots made no sound. "A few months ago I wouldn't have believed there could be that much wealth in the whole galaxy."

"The bigger lines are richer than nations used to be," Huerta said. "And they have to plan with centuries in mind. Research for the Supernova class was started more than thirty years ago. They'll be our prime carriers for the next twenty-five years, and research on the next generation of ships is already under way."

"Hard to believe," she repeated. It was a long way from the uncertain little world of *Space Angel* and her hand-to-mouth existence. And she was still wondering why he was so determined to impress her. They came to a multitiered area of glass-fronted enclosures, many of them illuminated and all of them empty.

"This will be a mall area of expensive shops, restaurants, entertainment complexes and such. There are five such areas in the ship, graduated according to the traveling budgets of the passengers in the various sectors."

"It's like a whole city," she said.

"Bigger than many. Fully manned, with a full load of passengers, this ship can carry more than ninety thousand people. Of course, the bulk of those would be traveling in immigrant quarters. Not quite as luxurious as this level."

"I can imagine," she said.

"Right now only a small section of this first-class level is occupied for this voyage. Then there's the bridge and engine crew, and, of course, the construction crews down in the cargo area. Only a few hundred people aboard. What would you like to see first?"

"You're the tour guide," she said.

"Then let's start with the bridge." He took her to an elevator that ascended along an invisible magnetic column through the mall and into a higher level. They got off in a corridor that was far more institutional-looking than the level below. Personnel in color-coded uniforms bustled about in a disciplined fashion. This part of the ship, at least, was fully staffed. Through open doors she caught glimpses of rooms filled with banks of instruments, all of them tended by diligent-looking employees. It looked like dull work, not that she had much experience with people who worked at steady jobs.

She braced herself for trouble when she saw the towering form of Izquierda striding towards them, a gaggle of ship's officers in tow. "Tomas," he said, without breaking stride, "I want to speak to you this evening after dinner."

"Yes, sir," Huerta said. To Kiril's intense relief, Izquierda had passed them without sparing her a glance. "That's the way he is most of the time," Huerta said. "He doesn't take much notice of people unless he has some immediate purpose for them."

"That suits me," Kiril said. "I don't think we'd strike up a real sparkling conversation, anyway."

The bridge was suitably impressive. The biggest viewscreen was ten meters high by twenty meters long, and there were others not much smaller. Two screens kept the alien settlement constantly in view. Another showed the TFCS, and a small one, Kiril noted, had the *Space Angel* in its sights.

"Why are you keeping watch on the *Angel*?" she asked.

"Regulations. All nearby craft have to be kept under constant observation. There were some terrible collisions in the early days of space travel, and we have more observation and warning systems than you'd believe."

"Not exactly homey, is it?" she said, scanning the three-level room with its huge variety of instrumentation. There were at least a hundred people on duty.

"That's not an adjective I ever thought to apply to a ship," Huerta admitted. "I suppose if you spent your life in one ship and knew everybody in the crew, you'd think of it as a home. Line ships aren't like that, I'm afraid."

From the bridge they toured the support systems, the junglelike hydroponics section, the complex supply system.

"If, say, somebody in engineering wants a machine part from supply," Huerta explained, "he just encodes his request over the ship's computer net and the part will be delivered from supply within ten minutes. It's entirely automated." Kiril thought about Torwald's supply room and machine shop; tiny, cramped, and crammed with the surplus of the *Angel*'s hundred-odd years in space.

They passed through the cargo section on their way to visit the engine section. A car running smoothly on a magnetic rail transported them the length of the ship. At a hatchway leading into a hold, Huerta stopped the car. "Let's see, this is Hold Two. Let me show you the inside." They hopped out of the car and he touched a combination on a numbered plate. The hatch swung open and Kiril blinked at the vast emptiness inside. The hold was almost as large as the one the *Angel* had ridden in aboard the TFCS. The hatchway opened onto an access catwalk. "There are three more holds like this," Huerta said. "This ship is designed to carry entire colony parties, complete with people, equipment, and livestock."

Across the corridor, at an identical hatch, a tough-looking security man sat in a guard post. That hold was marked NO ADMITTANCE.

Kiril pointed to the guarded hold. "I thought you weren't carrying anything this trip."

Huerta shrugged. "There's still construction going on. There may be crews working in there, or maybe it's not pressurized. It could be dangerous to go in there."

Kiril felt a sudden spinal chill. She knew, the way that she always knew such things, that Huerta was lying about the hold. Something important was in there and he didn't want her to know about it. She filed it away for later. They climbed back into the car and headed for the engine room. On the way they passed a small group of men in silver coveralls. Kiril's attention fastened on them, although she made sure not to be obvious. They were tough-looking and scarred, like the guard at the cargo hatch. They were the kind of men she used to see following Pao Lin and the other K'ang leaders in Civis Astra. "Are those some of the construction people you were talking about?" she asked casually.

"That's right," he said. "They're still working in this area."

Once again she knew he was lying.

As she had expected, the engine room was big. She was getting tired of big. This spacegoing city was just a ship, like *Space Angel*, in everything except size. Given a choice, she knew she would pick the *Angel* any day. At least there all the people were professional spacers, which was what she wanted to be. Huerta had showed her a whole infirmary for the sole purpose of coddling rich passengers through Whooppee drive horrors.

"Now you've seen her from one end to the other," Huerta said, smiling up at a thruster only slightly smaller than the *Space Angel* herself. "What do you think?"

"It's kind of hard to take in all at once," she said. "It's overwhelming, you know?" That seemed like a good, neutral line to take. She wanted to keep him talking, to learn anything that might be of help to her friends, and that meant not offending Huerta. She knew real flattery would be better yet, but she had never used it and didn't know how.

"It sometimes has that effect," he said proudly. Then he glanced at his watch. "It's time for dinner. All the ship's officers and line officials dine with the director in the main wardroom. That includes me, I fear. Come on, you must be hungry by now. I promise not to seat us too close to the old man. With luck, he won't even notice us."

"Sounds fine," she said. "I'm starved." It was true, she really was ravenous. It had been a long time since breakfast, and somehow she had overlooked lunch. She was also fighting a treacherous urge to like Huerta. How could she possibly like someone she didn't trust? It was an uncomfortable feeling.

The wardroom was a paneled chamber with low-key lighting and walls decorated with holos of famous Satsuma ships of years past. A single, long table ran down the center of the room, and Huerta found them seats several places down from where the director was deep in conversation with a senior officer. They did not escape notice entirely, however.

"Good evening, Tomas," Izquierda said. His gaze fastened on Kiril. "Aren't you from *Space Angel*'s crew, young lady?"

"I invited her up, Director," Huerta said. "I've been giving her the grand tour."

"I might have known," Izquierda said, "that you would find someone to show the ship off to, and that it would be someone pretty. Enjoy your visit, young lady." He turned back to his conversation. There had been no disapproval in his voice. It was hard to believe that this was the man with the killer look she had seen at the diplomatic function. But she knew that she was never wrong about those things.

Kiril barely noticed what she was eating. Izquierda's presence made her nervous, and the other officers at the table were not going out of their way to set her at ease. She was, after all, an interloper from a free freighter, even if she was there as Huerta's guest. She ate a lot anyway. In a way, she didn't mind her relative isolation at the table, because it gave her a little time to think about what she had seen. Izquierda was up to something, and it had been something to do with that forbidden hold and those men who obviously weren't construction workers. And, whether he was in on the plan or not, Huerta was covering for his uncle and was not to be trusted.

But what had all this to do with the aliens? There had to be some reason for hauling *Space Angel* and her crew all the way out here where negotiations were opening. Was it part of Izquierda's revenge or had he found some convenient way to fit one plot into another? She had known people who could do such things, back in Civis Astra. It all called for further investigation. When Huerta spoke to her, she smiled automatically and said whatever seemed to be most diplomatic. Her mind was elsewhere.

When the dinner broke up, Huerta showed her to her quarters. "There's no telling how long the director will be keeping me in his meeting," Huerta told her, "so I'll assume it'll be a long time. There's a lot more to see in this ship, but it's been a long day and I know you're tired. I'll see you in the morning."

"You're right," she said. "I'm exhausted." She scanned the room for something to clout him with if he should make the wrong move. Instead, he just bowed slightly and left. She was a little disappointed. He could have made *some* kind of move, even if it earned him a minor bruise.

The suite he had installed her in was lavish, as she had known it would be. She was already numb to magnificence, but the fixtures and appliances intrigued her. She had no idea what most of them were; there seemed to be no manual of instruction, and she wasn't about to ask. Apparently, rich people were expected to know what all these things were. There was a bar with bottles and dispensers. She examined a respirator that was attached to a tube set into the bar. She touched a switch and purple smoke swirled from the tube into the mask. She recognized the scent of a drug favored by certain lowlifes in Civis Astra. It was illegal there, although it was readily available in the dope houses. Apparently, not everybody went by the standards of Civis Astra legality.

She couldn't believe the bathroom. In the center was a walk-in tub big enough for at least a dozen people. The Spartan accommodations of *Space Angel* allowed only chemical baths, efficient but short on luxury. She had seen baths like this only in holographic entertainments about the lives of the rich. This she had to try. After studying its control panel for a few minutes, she punched in a combination. Water swirled in to form a rising whirlpool, capped with rich foam and pungent with scented oils.

She paused before stepping in. It looked big enough to drown in there. She worked up her courage and took the steps one at a time. When she was in up to her chin, she sat back on the padded ledge and admired the colored lights that played artfully beneath the surface. It had taken some real imagination to turn the simple process of getting clean into something so decadent. She had a sneaking, uncomfortable feeling that she could get used to living like this.

Maybe that was the point of the whole show. Was that what they intended from the first: to seduce her with the soft life, then make their proposal? Suddenly the outrageous bath wasn't so enjoyable. She got out and stepped under an air dryer, regretting that she had come here at all. No, that wasn't right. Something was going on in this ship, something threatening to *Space Angel* and everyone in her. Kiril had to find out what it was.

It was still only late evening. That meant she could get some sleep before she set to work. The skipper had told her not to go snooping on her own, but she figured that this was important enough to override her instructions. There was a timer in the headboard, and she set it to wake her an hour before the late watch was relieved. At that hour people would be sleepy and not at their most alert. She picked a spot on the bed to sleep in. Her whole crew could have slept in it without crowding. As on her first night in her cabin bunk, Kiril had trouble getting used to the softness. Here, it was like lying on air. But this bed was equipped with soothing music and some kind of soporific mist that helped her nod off. It seemed strange that rich people should need help in getting to sleep. Probably, she thought just before sliding under, it was the thought of how they got rich that troubled their sleep.

The timer woke her with a gentle vibration. Whatever the soporific was, it cleared from her head as she sat up, leaving her clear-headed and alert. She checked and made sure she had slept only four hours. It was as good as a full night's sleep to her. She felt rested and ready to go. Also, there was the extra excitement that what she was doing was a bit dangerous. Much as she had come to like the routine of life aboard *Space Angel*, she missed the occasional moments of heart-pounding do-or-die excitement she had known on the streets.

She got into her coverall and boots and left the suite. She had determined to carry out this part of her snooping without bothering to avoid being seen. Why should she? Nobody had told her she was confined to her suite until morning. The few people she passed in the corridors did not spare her a glance. It was as good as being invisible.

When she came to the deserted mall area, she had to change tactics. A single person crossing these completed but unoccupied areas might be picked up by surveillance instruments. She found an elevator and took it down. Below the mall area was another, almost identical. Below that was a third, and here crews were still working. She figured they must be working three shifts around the clock, but that worked to her advantage because she would be less conspicuous.

She got off the elevator on the level where the crews were putting up paneling. The layout was identical to those above, but here the materials were plain, functional synthetics. This level served the immigrants or the third-class passengers. She walked about as if she had some purpose for being there, and nobody looked up from whatever they were doing. It was working out. She was dressed as a working spacer, although her coverall wasn't white like theirs. The construction workers had stolid, workingmen's faces, unlike the group she had seen before.

Kiril began to make her way back, towards the holds. There were long corridors of small cabins and big, barracklike rooms for immigrants. Some of these had been fitted out for the construction crews, and she passed tiers of bunks where the off-shift workers slept or viewed holos to pass the time. All through this area, people were installing lights, putting in wiring or plumbing, all the tasks of fitting out a ship for space.

The living quarters ended at a bulkhead that separated them from the holds. She stepped into an elevator and took it up to the level of the access corridor she and Huerta had taken earlier. She didn't dare call for one of the transports they had ridden in, but the walk wasn't all that far. She moved very quietly as she neared the guarded hatch. As she reached it, Kiril knew she had timed it just right. The guard was seated at his post, sound asleep. She checked her watch. If this area were run on a regular ship's schedule, he was due to be relieved in about ten minutes.

She had been coached by experts on how to move silently. She leaned over the guard and studied the panel below his flat-vision screen. She found a pressure plate marked Hold Three and punched it. The screen lit up. Kiril just stared, unable to register what she was seeing. Inside, dwarfed by the immensity of the hold, was a ship. The ship was *Space Angel*.

Her mind kicked into gear again. How had they brought her aboard, and why? Then she noticed a row of slots around the ship's midsection she didn't remember seeing on the *Angel*. That was where the holds were. Delicately, she worked the viewer into a closeup scan of the ship. The shape was identical, the old, dust-scarred sides the same. The navigator's bubble came into view. She could just make out the banks of instruments inside. The *Angel*'s had been torn out years before. This ship was almost the same, but it wasn't the *Angel*.

Kiril knew that it was time to get out. Now she had something to take back. She didn't know what it signified, but finding this justified the risk she had taken. But there might be more. What else was in that hold? She found a numbered series of plates below a label denoting storerooms and access corridors. She began hitting them in sequence, viewing one empty room and passage after another, scanning each for a moment before going on to the next. Then she hit the jackpot. One was occupied. She spared an instant to glance at her watch. Her time was gone. She should clear out fast. She decided to press her luck a little further.

The storeroom had been rigged as a barracks. She could see at least three men stretched on bunks. Another had his head enveloped in a holoviewer. Two sat at a table in the center of the room playing a complicated game with dice and counters. The ones she could see wore military coveralls equipped with colorshift camouflage. One of the game-players reached across the table to place a counter, and she watched the arm of his coverall change from the brown of his chair to the green of the tabletop.

The men had hard, brutal faces. She knew this breed, all right: mercenaries who fought for pay in the little wars that had begun as soon as the big one was over. She had seen many like these in the streets near the port of Civis Astra. On liberty when their ships put in for fuel or repairs, they had been big spenders and valued customers in all the dives and dope houses.

She had the viewer scan the room, and she saw a rack of beam rifles. She could see that the weapons were unsecured. One of the oldest and most rigidly enforced rules was the one against letting anyone handle a weapon or tool that might pierce the hull of a ship in space. She wanted to see more but turned the screen off. Time to go.

The sleeping guard didn't stir as she left him. A hundred meters down the corridor she began to breathe regularly again. It looked like she was going to get away with it. Then a door opened almost in her face and a man stepped out into the corridor.

"Well, what have we here?" It was one of the mercs, wearing a ship's security uniform. Undoubtedly this was the sleeping guard's relief. He couldn't carry a gun, of course, but he had a stun rod on one hip and a sheathed knife on the other.

"I been back to the engine room to deliver some stuff," Kiril said. Might as well brazen it out. "If you're going on guard, you better hurry. Your buddy back there's snoring up a storm. Whoever's security chief on this tub won't like that."

His ugly, scarred face split in a grin. "You don't say. Well, if he's asleep, he won't notice if I'm a few minutes late."

"What do you mean?" she said, ready to bolt. Before she could even pick a direction, he grabbed her arm and yanked her into the access corridor he had stepped from. He sealed the door and turned to her, still grinning.

"What I mean is, anybody with a call to go to the engine section just takes a shuttle car. And when they want something back there, they just send for it through the delivery system. It don't need to be hand carried."

Automatically her hand went for one of her wrist sheaths, but her knives were still back aboard the *Angel*. Mentally she cursed herself. She had let shipboard life make her soft and slow. Back in the alleys this ugly lout would never have laid a hand on her. Old K'Stin would be ashamed of her, if she ever got back alive.

"You don't work on this ship," the merc said. "You're some officer's play toy he brought along, ain't you? Only you got a boyfriend back there in engine section and you don't want your sugar daddy to know when you go visit him. I'm right, ain't I?"

"You got it," she said. "Now let me out of here."

"Sure," he said. "Only before you go, you're gonna let me in on boyfriend's action, or maybe your officer friend finds out his dolly been taking unauthorized trips sternward."

She let him get his arms almost all the way around her before she took the knife from his belt and opened his uniform from belt to collar. Then she spun and cut from shoulder all the way to wrist. The merc jerked back, his face a ludicrous picture of surprise. His mouth dropped open as he saw his uniform ribboning away from his body and arm. A single, continuous cut ran from his belly to his collarbone, then made a right-angle turn and went down his arm to the wrist. Blood began to seep from the shallow gash as he watched.

"You cut me!" he said. Then he called her a number of things so shocking that some of them were new even to Kiril. "I'm gonna make you wish you'd been smart and agreeable."

He started for her, but she raised the knife and he stopped.

"That was a little scratch, but you could be looking at your guts right now and you know it, soldier." She hissed her words in a deadly monotone. "I can sure give you that look if you push this."

He started to grin again. "Just a little way down that hall is a dozen more men even prettier than me. If I just holler, you're gonna have to do some real fast cutting."

"Sure, soldier," she taunted. "You're gonna tell your friends that you let a skinny little girl take your knife away and cut you with it. No, I'll tell you what you're gonna do: You're gonna go to your infirmary and put some tape on that little souvenir I gave you, and you're gonna get into a new uniform. Then you're gonna go and relieve your sleeping friend. And while you're doing all that you better be praying that I don't tell Izquierda that one of his hired thugs forgot he was supposed to keep a low profile." It was the last threat that struck home. He had half smiled until she mentioned Izquierda's name, then his face held nothing but fear.

She sidled around him and reached behind her to grasp the door handle. He didn't try to stop her as she opened it up and slipped through, always keeping the blade between herself and the merc. She shut the door and started to run. She heard no pursuit, but she did not slacken her pace until she reached the elevator. Her heart thudded and she began to shake as the elevator dropped. She stopped it at one of the unoccupied levels and waited for the shakes to pass.

When she was more composed, she realized that she was still holding the knife. It wouldn't be much help if Izquierda's men came for her, but she didn't want to give up the only weapon she had. She searched an empty corridor until she found a scrap of tough molyfilm left by some worker. She wrapped the plastic around the knife and thrust the wrapped blade into the top of her boot. She bloused her trouser leg around the handle until she was satisfied that it didn't show, then got back into the elevator.

On the level where work was going on, she got off and retraced her steps. At every moment she expected security men to collar her and take her to Izquierda. When she reached her suite, she went inside and sat tensely for several minutes. It

meant nothing that she had made it here without incident.
Maybe Izquierda wanted to keep this quiet. It was fairly certain
that most of the line officers on the ship weren't in on his plot.
She looked at her watch. Still two hours before wakeup. She
knew she wasn't going to get any sleep between now and that
time.

6

When Kiril heard the quiet tone of the wakeup call, she knew that she had actually nodded off. It was morning and nobody had come to get her. Groggily, she got out of the chair and went to the bathroom to freshen up. She splashed icy water in her face and straightened her hair until she was satisfied that she didn't look either disgraceful or suspicious.

She went back into the main room. Nobody had told her what the breakfast arrangements were, but she heard a musical tone and saw a panel open in one of the walls. Inside was a tray bearing covered dishes. She took the tray to a table and sat. "They sure don't make you knock yourself out around here," she muttered to herself. She ate hungrily, noting that the food was really no better than she was used to aboard the *Angel,* although it was more elegantly served. When she was through eating, she sipped at the coffee. It still tasted vile, but since spacers seemed to live on the stuff, she figured she'd better cultivate a taste for it.

She set the cup down with relief when a voice came out of

nowhere. "All personnel on the landing party, report to the shuttle dock in fifteen minutes." The voice repeated the instruction and Kiril stood, pushing table and tray away from her. She checked to make sure that the knife was secure in her boot and not showing. She hoped there wouldn't be a weapons check before boarding the shuttle. She didn't dare leave it in this suite, but she didn't know of anyplace to dispose of it between here and the dock and she wanted to keep it, anyway. It was more than just a weapon now; it was evidence of a sort.

She took a last look at the incredibly luxurious suite before she left. A few months ago she had thought that only gods or holo stars could live like this. It was gorgeous and seductive, like the rest of the ship, and she wanted to be away from it more than she'd wanted anything else in her life.

Huerta met her at the shuttle dock. "Did you sleep well?"

For the first time in hours she felt a little safe. Surely they wouldn't try anything in this mass of people. "Never better. The setup here is a lot more posh than I'm used to."

"That could be changed," he said enigmatically. Uh-oh, she thought, here comes the pitch. Bewilderingly, though, he let it drop. Izquierda arrived and he signaled to Huerta. The young man went to join him, and he remained with the circle around the director for the duration of the trip back down to the planet.

The *Angel*'s crew had not yet arrived when Kiril got off the shuttle. She began walking toward the ship, then stopped. She didn't want to look conspicuous. Best to wait for them to show. There was no sign of the aliens yet. A few minutes later they arrived, and she went to join them.

"Any problems?" the skipper asked Kiril.

"We have to talk," she said in a low voice.

"Later," the skipper said, smiling for the benefit of anyone who might be looking. "Don't say anything until we're back aboard ship."

Nagamitsu saw them and signaled for them to join him where he stood with a knot of scientists. "Any luck with the language?" the skipper asked.

"We've made very little headway," Nagamitsu said. "The computers have analyzed every sound they made and come up with nothing. We were hoping Homer might have had more success. How about it?"

"I lack sufficient data," Homer said. "But I suspect that the vocal sounds are only a part of their system of communication. There are odd breaks and pauses in what seems to be an otherwise conventional speech mode."

"We caught the pauses," said one of the scientists, "but we couldn't make anything of them. Our holos didn't show any concurrent body language to fill them in. Of course, we have no way yet to interpret their facial expressions. Some kind of chemical signaling has been suggested."

"My own belief," Homer said, "is that they employ a mixture of speech and telepathic communication."

"Telepathy!" said the head of the scientific mission. "It's so rare that we have little understanding of it. If they really do communicate that way, we could have great difficulty in establishing a dialogue. Are you certain, Homer?"

"Not perfectly, but I have experience of other telepathic or part-telepathic species. The speech mannerisms of these people bear some resemblance to theirs. Perhaps today I can gain enough data for a key to their speech. I have only a very slight telepathic sensitivity myself, and in my experience it is rare that even two fully telepathic species can communicate efficiently. However, I think a mutual language can be established. If they did not depend upon it strongly, they would have no spoken language at all. It is not impossible that the telepathic signals carry only small but crucial inflections of meaning."

"Let's hope so," Nagamitsu said. "Here they come."

There were only three of the aliens this time. Two of them carried instruments of some kind; a flat, black box and a slender rod covered with odd markings.

"It looks as if they've come prepared to do some analyzing of their own," Nagamitsu said. "Homer, gentlemen, go to it."

Homer and three of the scientific party walked over to the aliens. They had recording devices and one carried a flat computer display screen. If the two species could not communicate directly, it was hoped that some kind of computer dialogue could be established. Assuming that the aliens had computers, of course. It was difficult for the humans to imagine how a species could accomplish interstellar travel without computers, but Homer insisted that he knew of several species that did exactly that.

They watched the scientists at their tedious task for several minutes. "Admiral," the skipper said, "this is a momentous event of great historical significance, but it's about as exciting as watching grass grow. If you don't mind, we'll return to our ship and paint the bulkheads or something. Let us know if something interesting happens."

"I envy your relative independence," Nagamitsu said. "Duty keeps the rest of us here. Go ahead, but keep your ship-to-ship hailer open."

They returned to the *Angel*. Torwald started to talk as soon as they were inside, but the skipper hand-signaled him to be quiet. When they were in the mess room, she turned to the rest. "They might have some kind of listening device aimed at us, and it'd look suspicious if we buttoned up the hatch, so no talking near the lock. Finn, check her for snoop devices."

Kiril stood motionless while Finn checked her out with an instrument that looked like a pistol to her. She hadn't considered the possibility that they might have planted a bug on her. "She's clean," Finn announced.

"All right, Kiril, let's hear it." The skipper sat, and so did the rest.

Kiril began her story, from the time she boarded the shuttle to the dinner in the officer's wardroom. When she got to the part about her late-night escapade, she said: "Sorry, Skipper. I know you said for me not to snoop on my own, but it just seemed too important, and the opportunity was there."

The skipper snorted disgustedly. "I have a hard enough time getting people to follow orders in this ship. It'd be too much to hope that somebody'd be obedient on another ship. Go ahead, tell us all about your spook mission."

Kiril told them the rest. She could tell from their expressionless stares that they weren't buying it. "I hope you realize," the skipper said when she had finished, "that that's just about the craziest story I ever heard. A duplicate *Angel* in the hold? Hired troops hiding in the supply rooms? Are you sure you didn't sample the goods in that bar in your luxury suite?"

Kiril took the knife from her boot and tossed it in the middle of the table. "The shops aren't open yet," she said, "so you know I didn't pick it up from a souvenir vendor."

The skipper frowned and picked the knife up. She unwrapped

the blade and handed it to Finn. "Anybody seen one like this before?" Finn shook his head and passed it to Torwald.

The quartermaster examined the curved blade and deeply checked, black composition handle. "This was made on Belisarius. I saw lots of troops from there carrying these during the War. Those rats changed sides so many times their boots were made with toes at both ends."

"So the part about the mercenaries is true," Finn said. "Kiril, I've known a lot of mercs. Mostly, they're just soldiers adrift after the War who don't know any other trade. Do you think the one you encountered was a rogue?"

She shook her head. "That whole lot's the kind that'll cut your throat for pocket change. Back in Civis Astra I've seen them knife each other in alleys for the price of a drink."

"He has them there for some kind of dirty work, then," Bert said. "But that part about the ship is still a little hard to accept."

The skipper was sunk in her chair, pondering deeply, her head almost buried in her collar. "I'm not so sure about that now," she said around her cigar. "Ham, what shape's our *Registry of Spacecraft* in?"

"I had it updated last year," the mate reported.

"Maybe that'll do us," she said. "I want to know what's happened to all the ships of the old Angel Line. I thought we had the only one still spacing, but maybe I'm wrong. Let's go see."

They trooped up to the bridge and crowded inside. Ham keyed the computer for the relevant information and watched it arrive on the screen. "Here we go: The Angel Line was founded in 2085, and the ships were built on Luna over the next ten years. First one was delivered in '86."

"We're not interested in how they started," the skipper said, "just in how they ended up."

"Let's see," Ham said. "*Angel of the Nebulae* collided with a Black Star Line ship in Mars orbit in 2127 and was scrapped as beyond salvage. *Star Angel* was destroyed during the Six Power War of 2110. *Venusian Angel* just plain disappeared during Whooppee transition." They all shuddered. Every year one or two ships went into Whooppee drive and were never heard from again. Spacer superstition held that the crews of such ships endured Whooppee horrors for eternity.

"*Angel of Sirius* was scrapped as obsolete ten years ago. Here's *Space Angel*, we know all about her. *Guardian Angel* was an armed ship, used for convoying the others in the early days. Lots of ship-to-ship piracy back in those days. She was sold off when the Angel Line was absorbed by Four Planet Line in '47. Bought by a state-owned service during the Sirius system settlement. Used for inner-system convoying at that time. Pressed into naval service during several emergencies, the last time being during the War. She was used as an orbital picket and saw no action. She was mothballed after the War. That's where her record ends."

"I'd forgotten about that one," the skipper said. "Let's have a look at her."

Ham punched the display control and an image formed in the holo tank. It had been made by some early holographic process and the image was inferior, flickering every few seconds. It was good enough to show all relevant details, though. It showed a ship of the same class as the *Space Angel,* and for the first time Kiril saw what the *Angel* must have looked like when she was new. *Guardian Angel* had the same bluntly sleek lines, but she was resplendent with blue and gold enameling. *Space Angel*'s enameling had been scoured off by more than a century of space dust.

Michelle pointed at the ship's midsection. "There are the slots around the hold area that Kiril saw."

"This is the one," the skipper said. "Kiril, I owe you an apology. You told it to us straight."

Kiril didn't know what to say to that. It had never occurred to her that people should believe something she said just because she said it.

"She was an armed ship," Torwald said, "so I'd imagine the slots are some kind of weapon ports."

"Now comes the big question," Bert said. "Just what does this all lead up to?"

"That has me stumped," said the skipper, "but I'll confess that I'm beginning to wish I'd let K'Stin take Izquierda out when I had the chance."

"Told you," K'Stin said.

*   *   *

There was no progress in establishing contact with the aliens that day. Once again they upped ship for the night. Kiril was relieved that she would be sleeping in her tiny cabin rather than in the palatial suite aboard the Supernova. She closed and, from habit, locked the hatch to her cabin. She was about to drop onto her bunk when she saw that it was already occupied by something green and furry. She squawked and flattened back against the hatch as it sat up and looked at her. A pair of bright, button eyes blinked at her solemnly from either side of a big, blobby nose. It was about two feet high as it sat with its stumpy legs curled under its nearly spherical body. It scratched in its belly fur with a forepaw that looked like a primitive hand. Enormous ears formed a bonnet around its placid face. It looked harmless, but Kiril wasn't taking any chances. She reached behind herself and got the hatch open. She heard footsteps in the corridor and knew by their sound that it was Lafayette heading back to the engine room.

"Hey," she called, "come here, there's something in my bunk and I think it must've got in from outside."

Lafayette barreled into the cabin, knocking her aside, yanking a heavy wrench from his belt. He stopped and stared at the thing on the bed, then put the wrench away, laughing uproariously.

"What's so funny?" she demanded. "What is that thing?"

Lafayette picked it up, and the little beast tried to wrap its stubby arms around his neck. "What scared you is probably the most harmless life form since the sponge. This is Teddy. He's a Narcissan Teddybear. It's the only life form known to have evolved lovability as a defense mechanism." He tickled it under the chin.

"You mean it's a pet? How come I ain't—" she corrected herself hastily, "—*haven't* seen it before?"

"He's been hibernating. Every couple of years he'll go off into a ventilation duct and sleep for a few months. That's why he's so skinny now. He must have awakened today and crawled out here through your vent. He can take off the grates and replace them."

"Skinny, is he?" she said doubtfully. Teddy was shaped like a ball, and she wondered what he must look like when he was fat.

"I'll take him up to the galley. He's probably hungry." He turned to go, and Kiril realized that she didn't want him to go just yet.

"Lafayette," she said impulsively, "what's the story on Nancy?"

"Nancy?" he said, puzzled. "What do you mean?"

"Well," she began lamely, "I mean, why's she so quiet? And why does she go off by herself to play that instrument?"

"You heard her play her violin? You were lucky. She doesn't do it often. There's not much I can tell you about her, except she was born on Li Po. I know you've heard of that place. She was one of the few who got out before the battle."

"Li Po. That says a lot." Like the rest of humanity, Kiril knew about Li Po. It had been a complete, although unplanned, planetary wipeout during the course of the most disastrous battle of a war full of military disasters. She had been unaware that anybody at all had survived. No wonder Nancy wanted to play her violin and cry sometimes. "Tor was a POW. Michelle tells me she had two husbands killed in the War. I guess most of this bunch has had it rough at some time."

"Achmed never talks about the War," Lafayette said, "and I think Bert lost his family in it. He joined the *Angel* from a refugee camp just after the War."

"How about you?" she asked. "You got a hard-luck story like the rest?"

He smiled sheepishly. "No, I was born on a Family ship, the *Rabinowitz Maru*. She was almost as big as a Satsuma Class One, but there were only so many berths. When we got old enough to hold a ship's job, we drew lots and the losers had to go out on their own. I volunteered to leave because I wanted to try ships where everybody there wasn't a cousin or something, and see planets that weren't on the Family route."

"How did you end up here?"

"We landed on Sirius V one day and I spotted the *Angel*. I was looking for a free freighter, because Family spacers don't like the lines either. So I walked across the pad and asked if she was hiring. As it happened, they'd just discharged their ship's boy and needed a new one. So I stepped into the job you've got right now."

"You mean the ship's kid doesn't automatically have to leave? Some of them stay on?"

"I was lucky. Achmed needed an apprentice, and I always wanted to work with the engines, anyway." He scratched behind Teddy's ears. Apparently, he had forgotten that he was supposed to be mad at her for accepting Huerta's invitation. Kiril stroked Teddy's head, and he favored her with a look of amazing dumbness. She just had to like the silly thing, which was what the quality of lovability was all about.

"Look, Kiril," he said hesitantly, "I wasn't trying to play big brother or anything the other day. It's just that, well, you're still new here, and the rest of us have lived in the *Angel* for years. It's asking too much for you to board that ship for our sake."

"You think I'm not as loyal as you and the others because I haven't been here as long as you?"

"That's not what I meant!" he said heatedly. "But we have some hardcase characters aboard this ship, and it seems wrong to me that the youngest here has to take the risks."

"Risks? We're all in plenty of danger. Don't think that I'm absorbing it all just because I got separated from the rest of you for a few hours. There's lots to go around." Teddy, oblivious of the dispute, reached out and patted her cheek. "Anyway, you'd better get used to the idea, because I'm going to have to go back there before long."

"What do you mean?" he asked suspiciously.

"They put that show on for me for a reason. They have a proposition to make, and they haven't made it yet. I figure they want me to sell you all out somehow, but I don't know what they figure to get from me. But pretty soon now, tomorrow or the next day, I'm going to get another invitation. Then you'd better make sure your gun's on full charge, because things'll start happening pretty quick after that."

He stared at her for a few seconds. "I don't like it, but I'll admit you've got more guts than most." He turned and carried Teddy out of the cabin. She locked the hatch behind him.

Kiril had barely gone to sleep when a loud clattering in the corridor outside awakened her. She sat up. "Looks like this ain't my night for relaxation." She cautiously opened the hatch.

Sprawled on the deck at her feet was one of the Vivers. He was groaning and a thick fluid was seeping from the joints of his natural armor.

Kiril hit the communicator beside her hatch. "Bridge! Whoever's awake up there, send some help down here! One of the Vivers is down and he looks bad sick."

"Which one is it?" It was Torwald's voice.

"I can't tell them apart unless they're standing together and I can see which one's taller."

"Stay there."

"Where do you think I'm gonna go, jerk?" she said.

A minute later Torwald was in the corridor with her. Behind him was the skipper, looking as if she had just been roused from her bunk, which was undoubtedly the case.

"It's B'Shant," Torwald said. He examined the swollen, seeping joints. "I think I know what this is. Where's K'Stin?"

"Get away from him." It was the senior Viver. He had come from his quarters into the corridor with the incredible silence of movement that always seemed to be impossible in a creature so massive. They backed away as he stooped over his kinsman. Without visible effort, K'Stin picked up the four-hundred-pound B'Shant and slung him over a shoulder. "I will put him in our quarters and stand guard outside, in the access room. I will kill any who come too near." He strode off as silently as he had come.

"What was that all about?" Kiril asked. "How sick is B'Shant and how come K'Stin's not taking him to the clinic?"

"He's not sick," Torwald said. "Vivers have two skeletons, endo and exo. B'Shant's young and still growing. Like any creature with an exoskeleton, they have to shed their shells periodically in order to grow. At that time they're vulnerable. Until his new shell hardens, a Viver is soft. You know how they feel about that. Any Viver is obligated to drop everything to guard a kinsman while he's in the soft state."

"Damn!" said the skipper. "Just when we're finally likely to need those two, they go dysfunctional on us. It's a good thing I have their beam weapons and explosives locked up. We'll just have to stay out of sword range. From now on the access passage to their quarters is off limits. Tor, see that everybody gets word. I'm going back to bed."

The next morning Kiril was given K'Stin's rations to deliver. The Vivers' quarters were located in a storage room aft of the rear hold. At some early period of the ship's existence, the room had been used for storing volatile materials and had a small access chamber as a buffer to separate it from the ship proper. Kiril stood well back from the hatch and pushed the tray in with a long pole.

"Here's your food, K'Stin," she said. The Viver said nothing. He stood before the hatch to his quarters with a sword dangling from a massive fist.

"Skipper says we land in an hour. Be ready to strap in when the warning sounds." Again he said nothing. Apparently, he was going to take the landing on his feet.

"K'Stin, how long are you gonna stand there? We might need you bad pretty soon. You heard my story about those mercs next door. Izquierda didn't bring them along because they're good company." Again silence from the Viver. Torwald had said that he had no idea how long a Viver's molting process lasted. The two might be out of action for weeks.

Activities on the ground had taken on the atmosphere of boring routine. As the *Space Angel* crew crossed the pad to the shuttle, they could see that the landing party was much smaller today, consisting mostly of scientists. There was no pretense of ceremony. Homer went to join the communication party and the rest went to Nagamitsu, who stood with Pierce and Izquierda, all three looking profoundly bored.

"Good morning, Captain HaLevy," Nagamitsu said. He seemed not to notice the absence of the two Vivers this morning. "It begins to appear that this expedition is going to be as boring as most scientific missions. Except for the scientists, of course. They're as happy and excited as kids with a new toy."

"Admiral," the skipper said, "being as how we're of no great use here, do you have any objection if we up ship and clear out of here?"

"The linguists tell me that they shall need Homer for another day or two. After that I have no objection to your going on about your business. Do either of you?" He looked at his companions. Pierce shook his head and Izquierda shrugged his shoulders casually.

"Then you may leave as soon as I give you clearance," Nagamitsu went on. "Of course, you are all under security seal. None of you is to speak of these matters when you return to human-occupied space. You will be notified when you are free to speak. Is that understood?"

"Sure," said the skipper. "What could we say anyway? We don't really know anything."

A few minutes later Kiril saw Izquierda speaking with Huerta. Torwald and Finn had wandered to the edge of the permitted zone and were scanning the distant forest with viewers. Everyone was bored with watching the aliens and lately had taken to analyzing what they could see of the flora and fauna. She was going to join them when Huerta came to her.

"Kiril, we never got to finish that tour of the Supernova. Since it looks like you'll be leaving tomorrow or the next day, would you like to come back up this evening?"

Kiril had a sinking feeling in the pit of her stomach. The last thing she wanted in the world was to go back aboard that ship. But this was important, and she might be able to do far more good in the middle of Izquierda's lair than cleaning up the galley aboard *Space Angel*.

"Sure," she said, as if she were overjoyed. "Let me okay it with my skipper."

She found the skipper and Ham seated at a small folding table, playing a game of bridge against Michelle and Bert.

"They're ready to make their pitch," Kiril reported. "I just got invited up to the Supernova again."

The skipper laid down her cards and took her cigar out of her mouth. She didn't speak right away. "You all saw how Izquierda didn't object to our leaving in the next couple of days. He's ready to make his move. It's too dangerous."

Bert spoke up. "Whatever's about to happen," he said quietly, "she'll have a better chance of surviving it in his ship than in ours." Kiril was startled. She hadn't thought of it that way.

"I agree," Michelle said. "But don't say anything to the others. They'll try to talk you out of it."

"Okay, Kiril," the skipper said. "I'll leave it up to you."

"I'll go," she said quickly, before she could back out. "If I find out when he's going to move, I'll try to get you some kind of word.'' She turned and walked away. She was glad Lafayette wasn't there to make a scene.

The day dragged on wearily, with occasional excited reports from the linguists that they were making headway. By this time Kiril was beginning to understand scientists, though. They got excited and happy when they discovered some new difficulty that needed solving. Things were breaking up and people were preparing to up ship when somebody spoke up behind her. "Hey, Kiril." She turned to see Ham standing there.

"I was back aboard the *Angel* this afternoon,'' said the mate, "and look what stuck itself into my boot.'' Almost hidden in his huge palm was one of Kiril's wrist knives. "Funny,'' he went on, "but I guess it don't have enough mass to trip the navy's detector, because I just walked under it and it didn't make a peep.'' He gave her his piano grin.

She looked about quickly to make sure nobody was looking their way, then clipped the knife to her left forearm and drew the sleeve of her coverall over it. She stood on her tiptoes and kissed him on his cheek. "Thanks, Ham. I won't forget this.''

His face turned serious. "You just be careful. We don't take to losing shipmates aboard the *Angel*. You get in trouble, get us word and we'll come for you.''

She felt a sudden, unaccustomed rush of tears to her eyes as she turned and walked away. She knew now that he was more likely to need help than she was. But she felt unutterably relieved. It was stupid, she knew. Izquierda had a big ship and who knew how many men, but a four-inch blade made her feel much safer. Well, why not? The little knives had saved her life many times in Civis Astra, and it was as hostile a place as Izquierda's ship.

She tried not to let her subdued mood show on the way up. She strove to respond brightly to Huerta's chatter and to look excited about the break in what had become dull routine. They dropped off the navy people and proceeded to the Supernova as before.

"I won't put you through the wardroom dinner routine again,'' Huerta said with an engaging smile. "You're in the same suite as before. Just order whatever you want over the comm. The kitchen is fully functional already. I have some things to attend to for now, but I'll come to your suite this evening.'' He turned and walked away. It sounded to her as if he were assuming a lot, but that didn't bother her. She could keep him at arm's length for as long as necessary. She sincerely hoped that was all she had to worry about.

7

The suite was just as she had left it. The carpeting was as soft as
she remembered. But this time the place looked even more
uninviting than before. She closed the door and something in it
buzzed and clicked. A prickly chill ran across her scalp.
Carefully, her face blank, she tried the latch. It wouldn't budge.
She was a prisoner. She wanted to scream and pound on the
door, but she figured she was probably under observation. If she
could do nothing else, she could at least deny them that
satisfaction.

She sat in the huge chair, and it molded itself to her and
began to deliver soothing vibrations. She needed them. Her
nerves were trying to give way to cold chills and she was trying
to suppress them. Quite aside from the fun the spectacle would
give unseen watchers, she knew that it would be debilitating and
she was going to need all her strength soon. She let the nervous
fit pass and discovered she was famished. That was better.
Things couldn't be too bad if she was still hungry.

She went to the dumb-waiter that had delivered her breakfast

last time and she touched a plate labeled MENU. A long list of
delicacies reeled up the screen. Most of the items she had never
heard of. She spoke into the screen, ordering some items she
remembered from the diplomatic banquet the evening this all
started. Then she added a few extra items: "Oh, yeah, send me
a key or something that'll open this door, and have a shuttle
ready to take me back to *Space Angel*."

A voice came out of the screen. "No problem with the chow,
kiddie, but the other items we can't supply. Nice try, though."
It wasn't the same one she'd had her run-in with, but it was the
same breed. The food arrived within minutes, and she ate it as if
she hadn't a care in the world, for the benefit of watchers.

She dabbed her lips with a damask napkin and wondered
what to do next. As long as she had lived on the streets in Civis
Astra, she'd never spent a single night in jail. She was sure that
most jails were a lot more primitive than this, but it was a
prison, nonetheless. She prowled around for a while, looking
for some possibility of escape. She was not surprised when she
found none. She wouldn't have been locked in here if the place
was easy to escape from. She wondered if her shipmates were
under attack right now, and steered her thoughts away from
that. There was nothing to be done about it, and it would only
cause her grief to think about it. Eventually she stretched out on
the bed. It was liable to be a long night.

When she woke up, she knew that there was somebody else in
the room. She made no sudden moves. It might be to her
advantage if whomever it was thought she was still asleep.

"Don't try to be clever. You are awake. Your breathing
changed, and in any case, I sprayed you with wake-up mist."
Uh-oh, that was Izquierda's voice. She was wide awake, all
right, mist or no mist. She sat up and swiveled her feet to the
floor. Izquierda was sitting in the chair, impeccably tailored and
with a long, tobacco cigarette between the thin fingers of one
hand. His booted legs were crossed elegantly and he regarded
her with an impersonal venom that turned her spine to ice. She
figured it was probably his idea of appearing amiable.

"I guess you're going to tell me what this is all about now?"
she said.

"As much as you need to know. I imagine by now you have

heard dear Gertrude's version of our little *rencontre* during the War?''

"She says you let a bunch of refugees and POW's get killed to save some Satsuma ships and cargoes."

"Accurate enough, as far as it goes," he said reasonably. "It was a business decision. Those people were not paying customers, and the cargo shippers were. As for their deaths, I didn't kill them, the Triumvirate forces did. That is what military organizations do in war, Kiril, they kill people. Ours did, too. You will notice that none of the surviving Triumvirate officers were prosecuted after the War for those killings. But *I* was singled out, by your beloved captain, for court-martial!'' For a second he let the wild-animal look show through, and Kiril knew that she hadn't been wrong the first time. She had to play this carefully. The man kept his beast leashed, but the leash was short.

"She says you divided your forces, too. They got wiped out buying you time."

He shrugged. "Service personnel are expendable. I expended them, that is all. Popular propaganda makes much of the value and sacrifice of the brave military people, but at the upper levels it is different. They are just numbers, counters in a game. Some are sacrificed for the higher goals of the game. Some die and some make it home. Usually, who does which is a matter of pure chance."

"Looks to me like you didn't leave it to chance whether you got out alive."

He smiled, genuinely pleased. "Yes, I'm glad you perceive that. The superior player does not allow himself to be a pawn. Instead, he weighs all factors in his own favor before going in. I was already a wealthy man working with one of the greatest lines before the War began. I protected myself with my wealth and influence. It's easy with naval people, you see. I received an important commission, and I secured the strongest personal support from both my subordinates and, especially, my superiors. Should any difficulty come up, as indeed happened, I had my flanks covered."

"Why is it so easy to get navy people to cooperate?" she asked.

"Simple. They all knew that once the War was over, naval forces would be cut to a fraction of their wartime strength. Even if we were victorious, most naval officers would be without ships. Those who cooperated with me and always looked out for my interest, received fine positions with the Satsuma Line after the War. Likewise, I was empowered to promise high executive offices with the line to those officers who secured lucrative shipping and shipbuilding contracts for Satsuma."

"No wonder you got to be a director after the War."

"Precisely. My activities during those years very nearly doubled the size of the Satsuma Line and made it by far the richest in all of human-occupied space."

"Things must be a little slow now, in peacetime," Kiril said. She wondered what this was all leading up to. Izquierda really seemed to relish this opportunity to brag of his accomplishments. For good reason, he probably didn't get to crow very often.

"It has been, but I'm about to remedy that," Izquierda said.

"What do you mean?" This sounded even worse than she had dreamed.

"In a few hours I am going to start a war with those aliens down there." He smiled triumphantly.

It took Kiril a few seconds to decide she had really heard right. "Are you serious? You're going to touch off a war? You must be crazy! What makes you think we can beat them?"

"Oh, I have no idea whether we can. In any case, I have no intention of taking part in the actual hostilities. I've already done my share of that for the line. No, you don't understand what the great corporations are like. They are very nearly immortal. Satsuma Line is nearly two hundred years old. It has gone through dozens of wars, and emerged richer from each one."

She felt a dismaying sense of unreality. This madman really meant it. "But those were wars between humans," she said, trying to be reasonable. "How could you profit from a war if we lose to an unknown enemy?"

"I've done my homework," he said, brushing a fleck of ash from his knee. "I have studied everything your friend Homer has told us about the civilizations at the center of the galaxy.

Besides, I believe in a certain historical inevitability. Intelligent beings want power and they want to expand their species. These creatures seem to have a technological culture very much like ours. The major obstacle between us appears to be language. We shall fight a very long and profitable war with them. If we win, we may double the size of human-dominated space. Plunder for everybody.''

"And if we lose?" Kiril asked.

He made a graceful gesture with his cigarette. "In that case, there will be tremendous opportunities for those who cooperate with the conquerors. With the proper attitude and precautions, a great corporation cannot emerge poorer from any war. The only thing that can do that is mismanagement.''

"So what's my part in all this?" she asked. Then she realized that this man trusted only greed. "Where's my percentage?"

Izquierda grinned. She thought it made him look like a skull. "Excellent question. When the navy confiscated *Space Angel*'s records, I made sure to go over her personnel's records. You have only been aboard a few weeks. You are ship's girl, the most menial of tasks in space. It could take you many years to work your way even into one of the lower offices. Turnover in the small freighters is notoriously slow.''

"It suits me," she said. She had to keep him talking while she figured a way out of this. Her brain worked frantically. This man was so terrifying that it was hard to think clearly in his presence.

"Oh, come now, Kiril," he said, amusement in his voice, "you're no old-time navy man like your friends Torwald and Finn. Nor are you a born-and-bred spacer like young Rabinowitz. What you are is a little guttersnipe from the slums of Civis Astra on Thoth. A few weeks ago your next meal was your most glowing hope. What do you know of the sentimental loyalties of spacers, or the realities of wealth and power?''

He leaned forward and said earnestly, as if it were truly important to him that she fully understand: "Kiril, I do not say these things to your disparagement. You came out of the slums of a squalid city. So did I. People born to fortune have no idea how important control of our fate is to people like you and me. And let me admit, you have impressed me. You are tough and intelligent and competent. I can use someone like you. I was most favorably struck by the way you handled that oaf down in the holds.''

Just take it slow, she thought, and don't show how scared you are. ''You found out about that, huh?''

''Oh, yes. You don't keep secrets from me in my ship. As it occurred, the fool's commander found him doctoring that scratch you gave him. The commander knew enough to notify me at once. I had the story out of the dolt in short order.''

''I'll bet you did,'' she said. ''He regretting his mistake now?''

''He is too busy for regrets at the moment,'' Izquierda said. He dropped the stub of his cigarette in a recess in the chair arm and took another from his tunic. Its tip flamed as he waved it. ''He is learning to breathe vacuum. If he should master that difficult art, he can teach the sleeping guard, who is keeping him company.''

''Sleeping guard?'' she said neutrally.

''Yes, the one who allowed you to peek into the hold and see the ship I have there. It's a pity that you have told your shipmates about it. It forces me to move sooner than I had hoped.''

Here was a possible edge, a tiny crack in his plan she might exploit. ''What makes you think I told them about it?''

He looked at her with calculation. ''I could find out.'' That threw a real scare into her. She wished she'd kept her mouth shut. ''In effect, it's immaterial, though. I have already set my plan in motion on the assumption that you did. It's the only reasonable calculation. Did you tell them?''

Might as well go for broke, she thought. ''Would I part with valuable information like that? I couldn't figure out what was going on, but I like to be aware of what's happening, you know? It comes of being raised in alleys and fighting for your dinner. You don't keep aware of what's happening around the corner, you can end up dead. Only, knowing about it and talking are two different things. You know to be safe. You talk when it's to your advantage.''

This time he smiled with genuine delight. ''I knew you were a kindred spirit, Kiril. You could be very valuable, working for me. I think now you're in the right frame of mind to hear my offer.''

At last. "I'm listening."

He blew a stream of smoke, which was immediately whisked away by a vent. "I've already told you that I'm going to start a war. But, of course, I don't intend for people to know that I did it. No, the blame is going to fall upon your Captain HaLevy.''

Oh, boy. "That's slick," Kiril said. "You get your war and your revenge at the same time. Neat.''

"Yes, elegant, isn't it? I killed the others, like squashing bugs. But for her I've reserved something more fitting. *She* is going to plunge humanity into an unwanted war. However it turns out, her name will be a curse throughout history.''

"You don't do things by halves, do you?" She forced admiration into her voice. "Now let's hear about me.''

"I need a witness. A witness from *Space Angel.* The others shall die, but you will be spared. You were, after all, a mere ship's girl, newly signed on to the ship. You had nothing to do with the awful plan, of course, but you had discovered it and you were locked up while it was carried out. You'll tell a most tearful story before the Great Court. You'll receive much sympathy, poor, innocent girl that you are.''

"Wait a minute! I don't like that. The part about the court, I mean. They'll drug me and put all kinds of snoops and instruments on me. No deal!''

He sat back and laughed gently. "Kiril, my dear, you still just don't understand. I can buy *anything.* You'll be expertly coached, to begin with. You shall have psych treatment to evade any drugs and override any instruments. On top of that, I'll own the people administering the drugs and the tests. The people operating the instruments will be taking my pay. I may even have the judges in my pocket, but that's not important, because they'll have to find in your favor with so much evidence.''

"You're asking a lot, for me to get up and lie right in front of the whole human race with my life on the line. What do I get out of it?''

He looked at her with those serpent eyes. "For one thing, you get to live. That wouldn't be the case otherwise.'' Her heart sank again. What hope did she have against this killer? "But I would rather buy people than coerce them. Mere fear often tempts people into hysterical acts. Self-interest, measured in terms of material gain and access to power, is something far more reliable, don't you agree?''

''If you say so.''

He waved his hands, indicating their surroundings. ''You've enjoyed living among these surroundings, haven't you? Quite a bit more lavish than what you've been used to, aren't they?''

''It's okay,'' she said. ''But I don't mistake it for what real power's all about.'' She was pretty sure she had his measure now, but she had to be careful. Play it too cooperative and he'd treat her like a tool. Be too demanding, and he'd squash her like the bug he'd mentioned before. ''Fancy rooms and nice food are fine, but stuff like this don't last. You've noticed by now that I don't order any booze or drugs. I don't like stuff that clouds my judgment. I figure you must've come to the same conclusion a long time ago. I can separate dreams from reality.'' She could see that Izquierda was trading on the similarities between himself and her. It might be a good time to play on that.

He smiled like a man who had just found the treasure he had dedicated his life to searching for. ''Kiril, you're even better than I had hoped. All right, let's stop fencing. I had planned to space this over a long time, enticing you with greater and greater exposures to the luxuries of the rich. I confess, I had thought that I was unique, that my clear perception of the world and the ways of men was something that might never be repeated in another human being. I was wrong. You are just what I was, forty years ago.'' He leaned close to her, being terribly intimate. ''I was once the chief of a gang, back in Buenos Aires. Yes, I'm actually from Old Earth. I was chief because I was more intelligent, and because I was the best with a knife. Never forget the importance of proficiency with the weapons, Kiril—without that, the most astute gang leader is helpless.''

''I'll go along with you there,'' Kiril said. ''You were saying that I was in for something a little better than a nice room like this and an automatic menu from the kitchen.''

''Oh, yes! I've determined that you have something far better in store for you than this, Kiril.'' He got up from the chair and began to pace. ''Kiril, I have more in mind than my own prosperity. The empire I have built means nothing without posterity; someone to whom I must pass my power."

"No kiddin'," Kiril said. "You got anyone in mind?"

"You have already had some dealings with my nephew Tomas. He is my sister's son. Her husband was not all I wanted for the family, so he is no more. Tomas, though, has potential."

"That's what I thought," Kiril said, sweating slightly. "I said to myself, 'this guy's got potential.' But his uncle calls the shots."

"Don't try to flatter me," Izquierda said coldly. Kiril nearly passed out. "Hear me out, and don't try to better your position in the meantime, is that agreeable?" he asked.

"Okay, shoot," Kiril said.

"That's better. I have founded an empire, and I intend to found a dynasty to rule it. Every dynasty that has gone before me has failed, because they have been too politically minded. They grew degenerate because they sought to marry their sons and daughters off to heirs and heiresses of various fortunes. That has always been a certain route to degeneracy."

"I follow you so far." She desperately wondered if he had remembered to lock the door. Should she try a break for it? What was the use? She was still in his ship.

"I think you're good genetic material, Kiril. A few months with the best tutors to give you a little polish, and you could be a glittering addition to the House of Izquierda. You have had a small taste of the good life, trifling, really. When you reach the realms which I inhabit, it's as if you had become a member of a different species. The old laws no longer apply, and there is no limit upon what you can do. You are utterly protected. Your slightest whim becomes the duty of the rest of mankind to fulfill. There is no longer anything above your reach, and you need fear no consequences of your actions. In fact, you may effectively banish the word fear from your vocabulary, except as a weapon to use on others."

"Just who was it you had me intended for? Tomas?"

"Most likely, but not necessarily."

"Or you?"

"Should I wish it. Now, make your decision, but make it quickly. I have a great deal to do before the night is over."

For the first time in her life Kiril seriously considered suicide as a way out. How fast was he? Could he stop her before she killed herself? Then she remembered that she had others to worry about. "I accept," she said, striving for an air of cool calculation. "How could I pass up an opportunity like this?"

"Wise decision," he said, getting to his feet. He stood within inches of her, so that she had to crane her head back to look up at him. He knew how to use his intimidating height to best effect. "And, Kiril: Never, never consider betraying me. Captain HaLevy attacked me openly as a foe and I spent a fortune and waited years for the proper moment to settle with her. That is nothing compared to how I deal with traitors."

She couldn't even get her throat to work for a reply, but she was proud that her knees stayed steady and she didn't faint. Then she forced herself to act calculating. That was what the man liked: calculation. "How will you pull it off?" she asked. "Why would HaLevy start a war?"

He smiled again. "Keeping your mind on business? I like that. Actually, that is part of your duties. You will testify how Captain HaLevy had been behaving erratically for months. You'll also have her secret diary, which will reveal that she was a raving xenophobe, appalled that humans were contemplating opening friendly relations with intelligent aliens. She was quite mad, of course."

"Nobody'll believe that!" Kiril protested. "That crew's the craziest combination of races and religions I've ever seen. She even has a pair of Vivers and an alien with her! How can you expect that story to stick?"

"Kiril, you have the basic material, but you lack experience of the world. You don't know how people behave in a state of wartime hysteria. They will believe *anything*. Besides, no matter how improbably, the irrefutable evidence shall be there."

"How is it I'm the only survivor?"

"I was wondering when it would occur to you to ask that. Come with me and I'll brief you as we go." He touched a control at his belt and a door slid open in a rear wall of the room. On the other side was a two-seat magnetic rail car. In spite of her predicament, she managed a wry smile, remembering that she had demanded to know whether the suite's door had a lock.

They climbed in and the car slid noiselessly through its access corridor. "My raiding party is about to mount its attack on *Space Angel*," Izquierda told her. "You are to go with it. There is little risk involved, since my men are heavily armed and the *Space Angel*'s weaponry will be locked up in the captain's safe."

"How'll you do it? Isn't the *Angel* being watched by the TFCS?"

"As it happens, the Supernova is between your ship and the navy vessel, and shall remain so throughout the action. By the time we lose that alignment, the real *Angel* will be aboard this ship and my duplicate will be in its place. I have fail-safe backup systems, of course. Some personnel aboard the TFCS who are on my payroll will be feeding a recording into the appropriate screen aboard the TFCS. Even should the *Angel* move from behind this ship, it will not be seen. A similar recording is being observed on the bridge of this ship."

"If you're bringing the *Angel* aboard," Kiril said, "why am I going with the raiding party?"

"I've given orders that all aboard *Space Angel* are to be killed before the ship is brought in. I except Homer, of course. He is far too valuable, and him I shall keep. I like an unequivocal demonstration of loyalty, Kiril. You are going to kill Captain HaLevy yourself."

8

In the hold, vacuum-suited men were preparing a small craft, dwarfed by the bulk of the former *Guardian Angel*. The car lifted from its magnetic rail and drifted on repellors to the side of the little craft. One of the suited men walked to the car. He saluted Izquierda. "All ready, sir." He was dark-skinned and his hair was roached in a scalplock. Most of the others looked like him. Stubby slug guns and knives hung from their belts.

"Then carry on." Izquierda looked at Kiril. "You'll go with Captain Lang. He may need you to furnish him with information, but stay behind, out of the way until the ship is secured. He knows what you are to do."

"What would you have done," she asked, "if I'd turned you down?"

"Then you would be dead, and I would have implemented a backup plan. I have several. Now get aboard that raider. I shall see you again within the hour, if you perform your duties properly."

She got out of the car and walked stiff-spined to the little raider. "Get in back," Lang said. She climbed in and walked past two men in shiny gray, jointed battle armor. Unlike the others, they gripped beam rifles. Three more sat behind them, in pressure suits with respirators dangling from their necks. She sat in a seat facing one of them.

The man facing her grinned viciously. "Hello, girlie. I just hope you give us some trouble. Old Carl'd still be alive if you hadn't cut him like that. We'd sure like to even things."

She leaned forward and put her face within an inch of his. "Yeah, well, I'm gonna be Mrs. Izquierda, so shut your yap and do your job."

He jerked back, fear on his face. "Yes, ma'am! Sorry."

Lang came back and draped a respirator over her head. "Put this on when we blast in. We may be making holes in that hull, and I doubt that that old hulk's self-sealer even works."

"How're you gonna get in?" Kiril asked. "They'll see you coming and they'll be ready."

"Not a chance. This baby's Satsuma's latest. It's got masking more advanced than anything ever used before. They'll never know we're coming until we're there. The director got her override codes from the navy, so we'll just open her AC hatch and drift right in. This baby's a raider's dream, and she's part of my pay for this job." Sure, Kiril thought, and the rest is the vacuum you'll all be eating as soon as you've finished Izquierda's dirty work. Lang went forward and took his pilot's seat. The lights went out in the hold as the massive hatch opened just wide enough to let the raider through.

Kiril studied her situation. Six big, tough, hardened men, two of them in armor. How could she deal with them? Well, the whole lot didn't scare her half as much as Izquierda. They were closing fast on *Space Angel*. Already she could make out the AC hatch they were going to use. It was where the atmosphere craft was stored, and it formed a secondary airlock that could be used in an emergency. She wanted, foolishly, to scream a warning to the ship.

Then the raider was drifting outside the lock and it was opening. The raider slid in beside the AC, the craft that had picked Kiril and Torwald up on Thoth. The outer hatch closed and the lock repressurized. The raiders pulled up their respira-

tors, except for the armored men, who wore helmets. "Out!"
Lang barked.

The raiding party rushed smoothly out of the craft and stood
with weapons ready. Lang went to the inner hatch and worked
its controls. It slid back and the three other men in pressure
suits rushed past him. Lang turned to Kiril. "Where are the
Vivers?"

She realized that he knew. He was testing her. "There's a
storeroom aft of the hold. There's an access chamber between
their room and the corridor."

Lang jerked his head and the two armored men trotted off. He
glanced at his timer. "You just stand clear, kid. It'll be over in a
few minutes."

She sidled up to Lang and, moving as swiftly and precisely as
she ever had in her life, lifted the slug gun from his belt and
spun away. "It's over now, clown! Call your goons off or I'll
splatter you!"

Lang grinned. "Well, looks like you aren't a loyal troop of
Izquierda's after all. I kind of suspected you weren't." He held
up his right hand. A finger bore what looked like a steel ring.
"That weapon's keyed to this ring, kid. Won't work without
it."

Kiril jerked the trigger. Nothing happened. Lang took two
swift steps and jerked the weapon from her grasp. He yanked
her arm and slammed her into the side of the AC. Kiril heard a
bone in her arm break an instant before a wave of nauseating
pain burst over her. She slumped to the deck, fighting for
consciousness.

One of the mercs came into the lock, herding the skipper,
Ham, Finn, and Nancy ahead of him. Seconds later another
came in, shepherding Achmed and Lafayette. Right behind
them was the third, holding Bert, Torwald, and Michelle at
gunpoint. Torwald looked at Lang and managed a bit of his old
smile. "Belisarians, just like I said. I didn't know there were
any of you left. What happened, did hell get too crowded to let
you in?"

Lang ignored him. "Where's the crab?"

"It's up on the bridge," one of the men said. "Just pulled
everything in and closed up like a clam. I couldn't move it."

"You left that thing up on the bridge?" demanded Lang. "With the controls?"

"I couldn't move it and hold this gun at the same time," the man protested. "It'll keep until we deliver the ship. It's just a big bug, anyway."

"Shall we go ahead and kill 'em?" asked another.

"Not till I know our situation. Where's the Vivers?" He called into a throat mike: "Shock team report. Report, dammit!" There was no answer. He glanced at his watch. "We're behind schedule. Listen, prisoners, we're all going to go check on my men who went after the Vivers. You people march ahead." He grabbed a fistful of Kiril's coverall and hauled her to her feet. "You, too. I don't leave anyone behind me."

"What did you do to her?" Michelle demanded. She supported Kiril from one side while Nancy took the other.

"She's suffering for being a fool. She had the greatest deal in the world and she threw it away to give you scum a break. Now march." They went into the corridor and headed towards the hold. A shuddering vibration went through the ship.

"What was that?" said the skipper, stopping. "What's wrong with my ship?"

"Nothing you're going to have to worry about," Lang said. "Now move."

The pain subsided a tiny bit, and Kiril assessed her damage. If she could just stay conscious for a few more minutes. She had only one thought: *Thank God it was the left arm.*

They came within a few feet of the converted storeroom. "Stop here," Lang ordered. He held his gun at the ready and pointed to Finn. "You. Go peek into that room and tell me what you see. No fast moves." Finn nodded and crossed to the door, which was slightly ajar. Very slowly, he stuck his head in. After a few seconds he withdrew it. His expression was distinctly shaken. "Where are my two men?" Lang said.

"Actually," Finn answered, "they're sort of all over in there. I hope you brought a mop."

Lang didn't change expression. "And the Vivers?"

"K'Stin's standing there with a heavy-duty beamer in each fist."

"There are supposed to be two Vivers," Lang said, his face a mask.

"B'Shant's probably taking a snooze," Torwald said. "Vivers don't get too upset over a pack of trash mercs, especially Belisarians."

With a snarl, Lang turned on Torwald, his finger tightening on the trigger.

"Wait, Lang," Kiril said. "We need to talk." She could barely speak above a whisper, but it was enough to distract Lang. She knew by that how desperate he was.

"I'm listening."

"Look, this thing has gone sour. You can't take this ship aboard the Supernova with a pair of beamer-armed Vivers aboard. They'll turn that tub into a junkheap in minutes." She staggered away from Michelle and walked up to Lang, her left forearm cradled in her right hand. "Look, Lang, give me a break. We can salvage this. Izquierda will listen to me. We'll say that my arm was hurt accidentally and somebody from the Supernova tipped the *Angel* about the raid. You cover for me and I'll cover for you. What do you say? I'm gonna be close to Izquierda, Lang. I can make it worth your while to help me out."

The mercenary gleam came into Lang's eyes. "Yeah, what're you gonna give me, little girl?"

She was close enough now. "This." Before the word was finished, her knife had gone in below his jaw. She had never used one to kill before, but she knew how it was done. She got it right the first time.

The merc who had spoken to Kiril aboard the raider reacted almost instantly, pulling down on the prisoners, but Finn's boot cracked into his chin just as Ham backhanded another merc onto a knife that Torwald had pulled from somewhere.

The last got off a short burst, but it was cut off when four feet of Viver arm burst through the metal bulkhead next to him and the spiked fist hit him with the power of a pile driver. All four men crumpled to the deck at about the same time.

"That man continues to underestimate me," the skipper said. "Imagine it, sending a half-dozen garbage mercs to take a free freighter." She raised her voice. "K'Stin, what's the situation in there?"

The huge Viver appeared at the hatch. Kiril blinked. He looked as if he had been painted red. "One of them managed to get off a shot before I killed him. I am sorry, Captain, I failed in my duty. A mere human, too. I shall be humiliated forever."

"You did fine," the skipper said. "Just be glad you've got forever to be humiliated in. Which direction did the shot go?"

"Toward the engine room," K'Stin said. The skipper looked at Achmed, and he hurried off, trailed by Lafayette.

Torwald looked into the access chamber and pulled his head out quickly. "K'Stin, that was just plain redundant."

"I do not often get to have fun in this ship," the Viver protested.

"How did you know where that man was standing?" Ham asked.

"Homer was observing from the bridge and told me where everyone was. My hearing did the rest."

Achmed came running back. "Skipper, we have a four-foot gash in number two thruster. Fuel is everywhere and it's getting hot in there. The *Angel* will start tearing herself apart soon. If we land now, before the thrusters get too far out of synch, we might have a chance. Or else we must abandon ship."

"Ham," the Skipper barked, "send out the distress signal."

"Don't do it," Kiril pleaded. "Izquierda has backup plans and he must have that covered. He'll blow us out of space. You've got to land now. He's gonna start a *war*! And he's gonna blame you for it—that's what the duplicate ship is for. We have to get away *now*!"

"Everybody back to the AC lock right now," the skipper said. She faced a comm plate. "That means you, too, Homer."

When Homer arrived, she laid it out for them. "I'm taking the *Angel* in. Maybe we can find a lake or something for a belly landing. I don't recommend that the rest of you ride her down. Whatever happens," she pointed at the raider, "I want that piece of Satsuma trash off my ship. If the *Angel* augers in, she dies clean." She left them with their decisions.

"I am too old to go about adventuring," Bert said. "I stay with the *Angel*." He left as well.

"She will never land without me to nurse the engines," said Achmed, heading for the engine room.

Lafayette looked at Kiril for a moment. "Kiril," he said,

''however it turns out, I'll never forget what you did.'' Then he went to follow Achmed.

Ham looked at the two remaining men and nodded. Torwald picked Michelle up and tossed her into the raider. Finn did the same with Nancy. Gently, Ham helped Kiril into the little vessel. Then he waved and gave them his big grin. ''I stick with Gert, as always.'' He left.

''Torwald, you idiot!'' Michelle said, as she checked Kiril's pulse. ''I can't pilot this thing and neither can Nancy. One of you will have to do it.''

''Get in,'' Torwald said to Finn.

''It's got to be you, Tor, me lad,'' said Finn. ''In case you didn't notice in all the excitement, I caught a ricochet from that merc's burst.'' He pointed to his thigh, where blood was seeping from a hole in his coverall. ''You'll have to run when you reach ground; get away from this raider. Izquierda can probably trace it. I can't run.''

Michelle tried to climb out, but Torwald shoved her back in. ''Don't worry about him. It always takes more than one bullet to kill an Irishman. I swear, Finn, you'll find an excuse to get out of anything. All right.'' He climbed into the pilot's seat. ''Button us up and close the hatches.''

''Saint Patrick watch over you all,'' Finn said as he limped out. Within a minute the inner hatch was buttoned up and the outer one open.

''Hang on, folks,'' Torwald warned. ''I've never handled one of these little babies, but what I lack in experience I make up for in enthusiasm.'' The raider shot out of the lock with teeth-jarring force.

''Why didn't Homer come along?'' Kiril muttered, barely conscious. ''And the Vivers?''

''K'Stin won't abandon B'Shant while he's helpless,'' Torwald said, ''and Homer can survive a ship crash.''

''There goes the *Angel*,''Nancy said. Through a port they saw the glow as *Space Angel*'s thrusters cut in, much brighter on the port side than on the starboard.

''That looks bad,'' Torwald muttered, ''but if anybody can bring the old lady in, it's the skipper. Right now we've got our own problems. I wonder what the aliens will think of us coming in like this?'' He chuckled. The man can laugh about anything, Kiril thought, groggily.

Torwald turned around in his seat. ''Well, nobody's shooting at us yet. Hey, how about the way the kid saved our hides? Kiril, that was the slickest—'' But Kiril was unconscious.

''Kiril, wake up.'' She could barely hear the voice. Somebody had her by the chin and was shaking her head. Managing to pry her eyelids open, she could see Michelle's face hovering above her. Behind Michelle she could make out some green, shifting shapes, but didn't know what they were. Michelle looked in another direction. ''She's coming around.''

Another face swam into view. It was Torwald. ''Kiril, how are you feeling?''

She thought about it for a while. There was a terrible, dull ache in her left arm and her stomach was churning. She felt feverish and just generally hurt all over. ''Not too bad, I guess,'' she said.

''I'm afraid it's going to get a lot worse,'' Michelle said. ''I'm going to have to set and splint this arm. That's why I had to bring you around. If you woke up while I was setting it, you'd probably go into shock.''

''There was an aid kit on the raider,'' Torwald reported, ''but no painkiller drugs. I figure the mercs were using them for recreational purposes.''

''Go ahead and set it,'' Kiril said. ''I been hurt before.'' A few seconds later another burst of pain put her under again. The next time she woke, she was much clearer-headed and the pain was at a manageable level. She looked around. She was lying under something big that sprouted a lot of fronds. She decided it was probably a tree. The ground she was lying on was bumpy and covered by some kind of soft growth. There were a great many odd smells in the air. All in all, it wasn't her cabin, but it beat waking up in Izquierda's ship. She risked raising her head. Nearby she could see the two women asleep on the ground. Torwald was sitting with his back against another tree, his head sunk on his chest. On his knee, his hand gripped a hand beamer. She wondered where he had found that, then decided it must have been in the raider.

Very carefully she shifted herself until she was sitting against the tree. She decided that if she could get a little food in her, she just might make it. Her surroundings were a new experience. She had never been in the open countryside before, at least that she had any memory of. There was a lot of noise: clickings, buzzings, chirps, and chatters. That made her a little apprehensive. There were animals out there, and they might be dangerous. She was glad that Torwald had found the beamer. At least she was alive. That had not been a likely prospect for some time now. And she wasn't alone. That made it even better. Things could be worse.

After a few minutes Torwald awoke with a start. He swept their little clearing with the beamer, then relaxed. He grinned at Kiril. "Glad to see you back among us, kid. What woke me up?"

"I sneezed," Kiril said. "There's lots of dust or something in the air. I never been out in the woods before. Is it always like this? It's kind of nice and peaceful."

"Every planet's different. At least we can breathe here. So far we've encountered nothing threatening, but that doesn't mean much. Back on Earth in the old days you could wander around a long time without meeting a tiger, but you had trouble on your hands when it happened."

"You think there's something here that might want to eat us?" Maybe this place wasn't so peaceful, after all.

"It's pretty rare that a species that's evolved on one planet can eat one that's evolved on another," he assured her.

"That's good to know."

"Of course, sometimes they'll kill you and only discover later that they can't eat you." He grinned. "But we'll worry about that when the time comes. As it is, we've got plenty of other things to worry us."

"Where are we?" Kiril asked. "Where'd you leave the raider?"

"We're about ten kilometers from where we ditched it. I kind of hated to leave it. It's a sweet little craft, even if the skipper has a dislike of anything Satsuma. Anyway, it might've been spotted by the Satsuma ship, or by the aliens."

"That merc captain, Lang, said it had some new masking process." Mention of the name brought her a vivid picture of the man's face. Had she really done that?

Torwald caught the sudden widening of her eyes. "Easy, kid. You did what you had to. We'd all be dead if you hadn't. You did all of humanity a favor. God knows how many that bunch had murdered over the years. It's done."

"Yeah, I guess so." She knew it wouldn't be that easy, though. "Did you carry me all this way?"

"Part of it," he said. "You staggered along some of the way. I carried you the last five or six kilometers. It's a good thing you don't weigh much."

Michelle was stirring. She smiled when she saw Kiril. "You seem to be making a fast recovery." She shook Nancy, and the comm officer sat up as well. Kiril thought that Nancy looked dazed. No real surprise there. She had lost her planet, now she had lost her ship. This is probably harder on her than on me, Kiril thought.

"What's our next move?" Michelle asked. "We've no idea where we are. We're stranded on an alien planet. We don't dare even try to eat anything here for fear of poison, and I've no way of testing anything. We don't know who's friendly and who's trying to kill us. We have to make some decisions fast."

"Not too fast," Torwald said. "That's been our problem, lately: things have been happening too fast. Kiril, if you feel up to it, how about telling us just what happened from the time you left us yesterday evening."

Had that been when it was? Had only a few hours passed since the latest installment in her nightmare began? "I'm up to it," she said. She went through the whole sequence of events, leaving nothing out. It didn't take long. At the end of it the others were staring at her in near-shock.

"I'd thought I was pretty hardened by this time," Michelle said, appalled, "but until now it never occurred to me just how awful one human being can be."

"He *proposed*?" Torwald said, a near-hysterical edge in his voice, as if he were about to burst into wild laughter. "He really wanted you to be Mrs. Izquierda?"

"Not exactly," Kiril said. "Not for him, particularly. He just thought I'd be good breeding stock. For him, or Huerta, or maybe somebody else in the family. He plans to raise little Izquierdas like thoroughbreds, just as bad as him." She tried to shut her eyes tightly, but she could not stop the tears from pouring down her cheeks. "God, I'm so ashamed!"

"But why?" Michelle said gently. "Because you played along with him? It was the smartest thing you could have done. It allowed you to get to us first."

"No, not that. He was standing there, closer to me than that merc captain was, and I couldn't work up the guts to make a try for him. I was so scared I just couldn't do it. I could've stopped all of this with one stab if I hadn't been such a coward."

"It would've been foolish to try," Torwald said. "He must be surrounded by protective systems. He could have had you killed before you had your knife clear."

"That's not it!" she insisted. "I was afraid I'd fail and he *wouldn't* kill me!"

"Kiril," Nancy said, speaking for the first time, "nobody could be asked to face a thing like that."

Torwald knelt beside her and put a hand on her unhurt shoulder. "Kid, since this business started, you've showed more smarts, guts, nerve, and loyalty than I've ever encountered in one human being. You can space with me any day." The two women nodded.

"Okay," Torwald went on, "we've got to assess our situation. There were no emergency rations on the raider, and we left the ship in too big a hurry to take any. We can maybe go another day or two without food, then we'll start to weaken. Then I'll have to shoot something, because it's usually safer to eat alien animals than plants. It's a desperation move either way, though. We've got to make contact with somebody, but who?"

"Our choices are pretty limited," Michelle said. "The Satsuma people will kill us on Izquierda's orders. The navy might do the same. We could be hunted criminals by now, if they really think we started a war."

"That leaves the aliens," Torwald said. "That's not as bad a prospect as it sounds. They probably aren't dumb, and they look as if they've experienced wars before. If they regard themselves as being at war with us, what they need now more than anything else is intelligence. They'll want to keep us alive for any information we can give them."

"I think we should try to find the *Angel*," Nancy said.

"I'd like to do that myself," Torwald said, "but we've no

idea where she came down. I brought us down within hiking distance of the alien settlement, but we don't know how much control she had. She might not have been able to bring the *Angel* down on this continent. Even if she's within a few hundred square kilometers of this place, one little ship will be awfully hard to find in unknown terrain. The aliens will find her first. I say we risk making contact with the aliens. Right now they're the only ones with a definite reason for *not* shooting us on sight."

"I hate to say it," Michelle said, "but you're probably right. A slim chance is better than no chance at all."

"I'll go for it," Kiril said.

Nancy thought for a while. "I guess so. They may already have the *Angel* in custody. If she didn't—" She couldn't say it.

"There's a little stream a few yards from here," Michelle said. "I'm going to go wash up before we set out. Kiril, are you up to walking, now?"

"Sure, I'm fine," she said. "It was my arm he broke, not my leg."

"Don't go alone," Torwald said. "Nancy, go with her. And don't drink the water."

"Who's the doctor here?" Michelle said. "I know enough not to drink untested water." The two women disappeared into the brush.

"Tor," Kiril said in a low voice, "will you promise me something?"

"What is it?" he asked suspiciously.

"Well, I wouldn't ask Michelle, because she's a doctor and she probably can't do it, and I don't know about Nancy. But you gotta promise me that you'll kill me before you'll let Izquierda take me alive!"

Torwald didn't turn a hair. "Sure, Kiril. You can count on me."

"Thanks, Tor." She could tell that he meant it, that he wasn't just humoring her. She felt much better.

Torwald helped her stand, and after a wave of dizziness, she didn't feel too bad. They went down to the stream, which wound among rocks at the bottom of a little valley. She studied it with interest, because she had never seen one before. She was used to gutters, sewers, faucets, and even the Supernova's bathtub, but she had never seen water running freely on the ground. She decided that she liked the sound it made. Gingerly she knelt and splashed water on her face, obeying Michelle's warning to keep her mouth and eyes shut as she did. She thought she saw something swimming in the water, but it was small and indistinct. The water made her feel much better, although she knew she was going to be thirsty pretty soon.

"Let me check your arm," Michelle said. Kiril's forearm was encased in a plastic splint, part of the raider's med kit. It had a loop to go around her neck for a sling. Michelle poked at the arm, frowning with concentration, but not with concern. The swelling had gone down somewhat. The splint itched and was uncomfortable, but not unbearably so. "It looks good," Michelle reported when her examination was over. "You can travel."

"I won't slow you down," Kiril said.

"Then let's get moving," Torwald said. He looked at his wrist chrono, which had a built-in compass. "We came down directly north of the alien settlement. This planet has a radical angle of declination, but I've adjusted for that. As long as we don't get killed in some violent fashion, I should be able to bring us out right on target. It's not far enough for us to starve along the way. Everybody ready? Let's go." He stepped across the little stream, followed by Nancy, then Kiril. Michelle came last.

"Keep your eyes open," Torwald said, "and remember that little bugs can kill you as dead as big carnivores. Plants can be predators, too. And watch your step, I've been places where animals used pit traps. We'll steer clear of overhead branches where we can. On Chronus there's a critter called a reatador. It looks like a big spider and sits up in the branches of tall trees. It catches animals or people on the ground by throwing a noose around them and hauling them in."

"You're doing wonders for my nerves, Tor," Kiril said. "Back in Civis Astra all I had to worry about was my fellow humans."

"Don't worry," Torwald assured her. "You'll never encounter anything anywhere that's *that* dangerous."

The woods were fairly open, with trees regularly-spaced but not so orderly that they looked as if they had been planted. The trees mostly had smooth, green trunks, but Michelle told Kiril that trees on Earth mostly had thick bark that was brown or gray. Most of the vegetation was green, but it was a different green than on the plants she had seen in hydroponics. Once in a while they saw small animals, but they never got a good look at them. The animals were shy and darted away as soon as they saw the humans.

"These things we're seeing don't act very dangerous," Kiril said hopefully.

"They wouldn't be skittish like that if they weren't afraid of attack," Torwald said. "There are predators around here someplace. But don't worry, me and my little beamer here will protect us." Kiril thought she could hear a disgusted snort from Michelle.

They managed to cover a few kilometers before darkness forced a halt. Kiril was relieved when they did stop. Despite her promise not to slow them down, she was far from being in top condition. Besides, she had found that a lifetime of dealing with streets, alleys, and rooftops had ill-prepared her for this kind of cross-country travel. It was not only tiring, but bewildering, and it left her in a state of confusion. She had never learned to get her bearings from things like landmarks or the sun. For all she knew, they were going in circles, and that was undoubtedly what she would have been doing had she been alone. Torwald had experience in the wilds of a great many worlds, and the other two women were not inexperienced at this kind of travel. Kiril didn't like to feel incompetent at anything.

She knew, though, that she was a quick learner, and that should she live long enough, she could be as good as Torwald. She listened closely to everything he said, even when he seemed to be bragging or just rambling on to hear himself talk. She had discovered that he seldom spoke idly.

"We'll have to do without a fire," Torwald said. "We have no idea what kind of sensors are trained on this area. We don't want to be spotted by the navy or Izquierda, and I'd prefer to make contact with the aliens on our own terms."

"The navy and the Satsuma ship may not be up there, you know," said Nancy. "They may be gone. If a war has really started, they may have fled back to Earth. Or the aliens may have destroyed them."

"I don't know," Torwald said uncomfortably, "ships the size of the TFCS and the Supernova—surely if they'd blown, we'd have seen some kind of aerial display. They were in a low orbit."

"We've been asleep," Michelle pointed out. "And we don't know what kind of weapons the aliens might have. Maybe nothing so crude as big explosions. How could Izquierda be such a fool as to get us into a war with an enemy whose powers are completely unknown? Quite aside from the injustice of it, the sheer folly is beyond belief!" She sat on the ground, hugging her knees.

"Even the most superficial study of history," said Torwald in his most inimitably pedantic manner, "shows innumerable instances of precisely the same kind of folly. What is usually behind it is either fear, hysteria, or, more commonly, greed and a desire for power. I would say that Izquierda suffers from a double dose of the last two. I'll admit it's a little unusual to find all that evil rolled up in one man, but it's not unprecedented. Ordinarily it's more of a collective phenomenon." He crossed his arms and leaned back against a tree trunk. Immediately he sprang away with a bitten-off curse. "This thing's got some kind of acid in its sap!" He rubbed the back of his neck.

"So speaks our dauntless woodsman," Michelle said. "Come here, I have some alcohol swabs in this kit. Now we can all sit and watch to see if you break out in purple blotches." She dabbed at his neck with a swab. "You have a nice start on some inflammation, all right. If that was a contact poison, we may have some real trouble on our hands. I wish you'd follow your own advice for once."

"Do I have to think of everything? I have enough problems looking after you helpless women. Ouch!" She had poked the center of his inflamed neck with a sharp fingernail.

"We might as well get some sleep," Michelle said. "Tor, you take first watch. That burn on your neck would keep you awake anyway."

"You're all heart, Michelle," he said.

"I'll take the next watch," she went on. "Nancy, you take the third. Kiril needs sleep more than the rest of us, so wake up Tor when you're sleepy."

"I don't need to be babied," Kiril protested. She had lain

down, exhausted, on a relatively soft patch of the grasslike growth. "I can stand my own watch," she mumbled, but she was already dropping off into sleep.

She woke feeling stiff. It was still dark. She sat up, suppressing a groan. Living aboard ship had made her soft, she decided. This ground was a lot softer than a doorway or a litter-covered basement floor, but it had left her feeling sore. Of course, back in Civis Astra she had never slept with a broken arm. Not that she'd lacked for savage batterings, though. She remembered one especially bad winter when she was twelve and got mixed up in somebody else's gang fight. A booted foot had cracked three of her ribs and she'd dragged herself to an itinerant healer-monk to have a gashed knee stitched. The following cold days and nights had been bad, indeed. All in all, she reflected, she had little cause for complaint about her changed situation. At least, for the first time in her life, she had somebody to share her misery.

"You awake?" came a whisper. It was Nancy.

"Yeah." She sidled over to where Nancy sat. "You been on watch long?"

"About an hour. No trouble so far. Just night-animal sounds. They can get pretty scary, though. There's something out there that screeches like a lost ghost about every fifteen minutes. I thought I'd had a heart attack when I first heard it."

"I must have been sound asleep," Kiril said. "I didn't hear a thing." They sat in silence for a few minutes, listening to the faint breeze stirring through the trees. Now and then they could hear animals moving stealthily through the foliage. There was a large moon rising over a range of hills to the east. It spilled a faint, bluish light into their small clearing. Once in a while they saw things with membranous wings flying between themselves and the source of the light.

"I've been on a lot of worlds," Nancy said at last, "but this is one of the prettiest. Most of them are either ugly or dangerous. If the aliens hadn't been here first, this would have been a prime world for colonizing."

Kiril wanted to keep her talking. "Do you think that's why the aliens are here? Are they that much like us?"

"We can't know yet, but I hope it's that way. It looks like our chances of survival are going to depend on communicating with them somehow. But how can we do that when all those scientists couldn't figure out their language?'' Nancy slumped back disconsolately. "I wish we had Homer with us. He knows his way around. Mostly I wish we knew what happened to the *Angel*. If she crashed and they're all dead, I don't think I'll live through it, not again.''

Kiril gripped Nancy's hand with her working one. "You don't make it if you start giving up ahead of time," she said. "Let's just stay alive for now, and we'll handle the *Angel's* problems when we know more.''

The big moon cleared the hills. Its surface looked smooth and was bluish in color except for a broad, golden band running diagonally from an upper edge almost to the center of the orb. "You're right, though," Kiril said. "It *is* a pretty place."

9

"Stand still," Torwald said. They froze. The sun was high and it was getting hot. They were all suffering from a fearful thirst. Hunger was bothering them, but the thirst was far worse. They had all but stopped talking except when it was necessary. Talking and dry throats didn't go together.

"In front of us, about thirty feet," Torwald croaked. "It's something I don't like the look of." Kiril's gaze followed his pointing finger. Something was crossing the faint path they had been following. Kiril had seen pictures of snakes, and this looked a little like one. It was about twenty feet long and two feet thick, but unlike a real snake, it moved on innumerable tiny legs. Its head was no bigger around than the body, and it tapered to a long, pointed snout. The head turned to face them, and they saw that it had no eyes. It was aware of them somehow, nonetheless. Its long snout opened to reveal a mouthful of long, thin teeth and an interior that was bright red, in startling contrast to its slate-gray exterior. It released a prolonged hiss, then turned and made off, moving with incredible speed on its profusion of little legs.

With a sigh of relief, Torwald lowered his beamer and stuck it in his belt. "That was a predator, all right. I'm glad it didn't think we were food. It looked too brainless to die quick."

"Let's take a break," Michelle said, the words paining her cracked lips. "My feet are sore."

"Haven't I always told you how important good boots are to a spacer?" Torwald said.

Michelle sighed as she slumped to the ground. "Yes, Tor, you've told us." Torwald's belief in good footwear rivaled some religions for fervor.

"You never know when you may be set afoot," he reminded them.

"We know that," Nancy said.

"As has, indeed, happened in our case."

"Tor," Michelle said, "will you kindly shut up? I'm too dry to chew you out."

"You see, kid?" he said to Kiril. "This is what they mean when they refer to a prophet without honor." The last words were so faint that she could barely make them out. Then she felt something. It was something she had felt at the edge of her perceptions most of her life, but so faint that she was never really sure that it was there. It was strong this time.

"Sshh," she hissed. "We're not alone!" She was as sure of it as she had been of anything in her life.

Torwald looked around, searching the nearby growth for movement. There was nothing to be seen. He strained his ears, as did the others. Nothing. "Hunger's getting to you, kid," he said. "We're all alone here. Just rest a few minutes, you'll be okay."

"They're nearby," she said fiercely.

"Who?" Michelle asked.

"I don't know, but there's a bunch of them."

Nobody seemed willing to give her feeling much credence. They rested for ten minutes, then Torwald said: "On your feet. The sooner we get there, the sooner we have a chance of getting out of this. Not much of a chance, I grant you." They set off again and within ten more minutes they stumbled upon the aliens.

Torwald saw them first. "Freeze." He stood stock-still, his

hands well away from the beamer. "Keep your hands well out and open. They use hand weapons, so they probably have a similar gesture."

The first alien stood in their path, about fifty yards ahead. He saw them a moment later and stopped abruptly. He said something rapidly, not to them but to someone behind him. In seconds five more aliens stood beside him. They advanced on line, in a decidedly military-looking fashion.

"Just be still," Torwald said. "Don't say or do anything. We keep quiet until we have some idea what our status is."

These aliens looked a little different from those who had conferred with the scientists. They wore coveralls of some shimmery, green-tinged fabric. It had a metallic sheen. They also wore flexible boots, and their harnesses were equipped with a number of strange-looking tools and what might have been weapons. None of them held weapons openly, but something in the way they held their arms suggested that some small objects bound to their forearms might be weapons. Their attitude was definitely not friendly.

"Uh-oh, folks," Torwald muttered, "it looks like it's wartime."

The aliens stopped when they were about fifteen feet from the humans. One of them, not the one who had spotted them first, barked some words, punctuated with gestures of pointing at the ground. "I hope that means he wants us to down weapons," Torwald said, "because that's what I'm about to do." Very slowly he lowered one hand to his belt. With thumb and forefinger he drew the beamer from his belt in slow motion. With infinite slowness he lowered himself and laid the weapon on the ground. Then he stood and held his hands out once more. Throughout this ritual he was careful not to smile. What was a gesture of goodwill to humans might be a teeth-baring threat to another species.

The lead alien made a peremptory gesture. He used the back of his hand instead of a finger, but he plainly wanted them to step back, away from the weapon. They did so, and the leader muttered something to his team. One of the aliens stepped forward and crouched by the beamer. He studied it for several minutes from a number of angles. At last he drew on a pair of gloves and took a small bag from a large pouch at the rear of his harness. Very gingerly he picked up the beamer and put it in the bag, then sealed the bag and placed it in his pouch. The alien leader pointed at the knife at Torwald's belt, and he shed that as well. Kiril unclipped her wrist knife and did the same. These weapons the aliens did not accord the caution they had shown with the beamer. The same alien as before simply wrapped them in some kind of fabric and stowed them in his pouch. At no time did he touch these objects with his bare fingers.

On instructions from the leader, three of the aliens rushed behind them. The leader and another flanked them and the last took point. Thus escorted, they set out to the south again. The aliens moved at an easy pace, and there was no prodding of the humans. On the contrary, the aliens did not seem to want to come closer than necessary.

"These boys are smart," Torwald said. "And they're tightly disciplined. At least they aren't likely to do anything hasty." He glanced at the leader, but the leader made no gesture that he should stop talking.

"You saw the way that alien handled the gun and the knife," Michelle said. "The gun he was cautious with because he didn't know what it might do. The knives he wrapped before touching as well. They must have standing precautions to take against contagion."

"Remember, whatever happens," Torwald warned, "it was us that started the war. It may have been Izquierda's plot, but humans attacked aliens, not the other way around. It's up to us to prove to them that our intentions are peaceful."

"I wish we had something to call them besides 'aliens,'" Kiril said. "I mean, Homer's an alien. They'd seem more like people if we knew what to call them."

"Very true," Torwald said. "I'll bet, right now, the guys in that navy ship have already coined some disparaging name for them. Happens every time in war."

"We have to get this war called off," Michelle said. "It would be terrible if humanity's first encounter with another intelligent species started in war."

With that they were all at last too dry to speak at all. The aliens herded them for another hour, then they came into a valley that had an odd shimmer to it. It was something like looking into a heat haze. The point alien walked into it and he began to shimmer, too. Then they were all through it and they saw that the haze had been camouflage for a small installation. A half-dozen small buildings dotted the bottom of the valley. The buildings were strangely irregular in shape, but there was a businesslike, military-seeming arrangement to the whole complex. At intervals around the facility were what looked like dug-in weapon emplacements, although they could see nothing that definitely looked like a weapon.

As they passed the emplacements, aliens stuck their heads out of bunkers and showed a very human-looking astonishment at the spectacle of captive humans being herded into their encampment. They were led to a low hut near the center of the installation. The leader pointed into the low-arched doorway with the back of his hand. Ducking, they went inside.

The interior of the hut was dim, but some thin panels on its upper surface admitted sunlight. It was cool inside, and the floor was ground covered with the mossy "grass" that carpeted most of the ground here in the woods. They sat, sighing with relief, as a guard was posted at the door. The rest of their escort left. Torwald examined the side of their little prison. Its surface was strangely irregular, with occasional tiny holes through it for ventilation. The skylights were formed from thinnings of the material, forming a translucent, parchmentlike material.

"What kind of prefab is this?" Torwald mused in a whisper.

Two aliens came into the hut. These looked more like the ones that had conferred with the scientists. They wore only harnesses loaded with instruments and odd tools. Most of these items, while differing radically, had an irregular appearance reminiscent of the hut they were in. The newcomers signaled the prisoners to move to the rear of the hut. When the order had been complied with, the aliens took fist-sized bulbs from their belts and sprayed the prisoners with a fine mist from head to foot, signaling them to turn so as to get all sides.

"They're medics," Michelle croaked. "We're being disinfected."

"Then these are the boys to ask about some water," Torwald said. He turned to an alien and stuck out his swollen, dry tongue. He gestured as if he were drinking from a glass, then he got onto one knee and mimed scooping up water and drinking. One of the aliens spoke to a guard outside and the guard left.

With other instruments the aliens took readings. They pasted tiny, thin patches on the prisoners' skin and took skin scrapings, which they carefully stored away. Having sprayed the humans, they now showed no hesitation at touching them.

Within a few minutes the guard returned and handed a large flask inside. One of the medics took it and handed it to Torwald. He looked at it suspiciously. "I hope they didn't just dip this up from a stream." He held out the flask and made a number of finger gestures around it, trying to convey the idea of a great many wiggly little things swimming around in it.

One of the medics jerked his chin forward two or three times. With extremely graceful and precise gestures, he held a hand over the flask. His fingers described wavy, rising motions, then his hand floated across horizontally. He closed his fist rapidly twice, then his fingers descended rapidly, wiggling to simulate falling drops.

"Evaporation, condensation, and precipitation," Michelle said. "He's telling us this water has been distilled!"

Torwald took a drink and paused for a few seconds. "Tastes fine," he reported. He handed it to Nancy. "Here. Beats dying of thirst."

She drank briefly and handed the flask to Kiril. Kiril took a grateful swallow and passed it on to Michelle. They all knew better than to gulp it down. They would sip at the flask for an hour or so, if their captors permitted it.

The medics stayed busy for another hour, taking blood samples, hair samples, and anything else that seemed likely to yield any useful data without doing serious damage to the subjects under examination. In all, they behaved precisely as human biologists might have, except for the strangeness of the instruments. When they took blood samples, they did not use a needle, but instead attached a limpetlike mollusk to the skin. It was pulled away a minute later, leaving only a tiny puncture on the skin.

"Amazing," Torwald said after they had left. "All those scientists with their computers tried for days to establish some sort of communication and came up with nothing. We got a lot of information across both ways with a little makee-pidgin sign language. I guess it just goes to demonstrate the innate superiority of free traders over all other breeds."

"I'll be even more impressed if you can find us some food," Kiril said. Now that thirst had been taken care of, she was far more aware of hunger. For some time now she had been accustomed to eating regularly. It was habit-forming.

"Don't expect anything too soon," Michelle said. "They seem to be quite careful. They'll analyze those samples they took and evaluate their data before they risk feeding us anything. The chances we can digest and metabolize what they eat is extremely slim. They evolved on another planet entirely."

"I was wondering about those instruments of theirs," Torwald mused aloud. "They didn't seem to be made of metal or glass or any synthetic I'm familiar with. The shapes were the kind you can make with extruded plastics, but they looked more like wood or bone."

"Look at this," Nancy said. She was lying on her side, scraping dirt away from the bottom of the wall.

"Hey," Torwald said, "we don't want them thinking we're trying to escape. That's the last thing we want to do. We need to stay put and act friendly and cooperative."

"I said come look at this. I was trying to see how they have this hut attached to the ground. Look." They all bellied down. The barky wall merged with the ground without a seam. Nancy had scraped away the soil to a depth of about two inches. An inch below the ground level the wall subdivided into thousands of thin, hairy fibers which gripped the soil.

"Those are roots," Michelle said disbelievingly. "This thing *grew* here."

"Are they taking advantage of a local resource," Torwald said, "or did they bring this?"

"This thing was designed as a dwelling for creatures the size of the aliens or us," said Nancy. "It wouldn't have evolved here."

"Then this is a product of gene manipulation," Torwald said. "Do you think they grew their instruments as well? That would explain their organic look."

"If so," said Michelle, "then their level of plant manipulation is immensely greater than ours. We usually have to completely rebuild the soil of a new planet before we can get Earth-evolved plants to grow there. These people can go out in the wilds of a new world and grow their own houses."

"They have to make some use of metals," Torwald said. "They have spacecraft, and vegetable fibers make notoriously poor conductors. And the head alien back at the start of negotiations wore a dagger."

"It was sheathed, we didn't see the blade," Michelle reminded him.

"They have to use metals and glass and synthetics," Torwald insisted stubbornly. "Otherwise they never could have developed an advanced technology and gotten into space. It just doesn't make sense."

"Since when," said Michelle, "is it incumbent upon the universe to make sense to you? Don't you remember our trip to the center of this galaxy? How much of that made sense?"

"Very little. But it might've if we'd had a closer look."

They went on in this vein for some time. Kiril got tired of listening and went to the door to see if anything was going on outside. She sat cross-legged in the doorway to make it plain that she wasn't trying to make a break for it. There was only one guard there, sitting, or rather squatting, next to the door. He appeared at first glance to be unarmed, but now that she had leisure, she looked closely at the complex of little tubes and bumps strapped around his forearm. Some of them ended in open muzzlelike holes just above his wrists. They were almost certainly weapons.

She took a deep breath. "Hello," she hazarded. The guard swiveled his head to look at her. His mouth crooked up at one corner and down at the other. She hoped that was the equivalent of a friendly smile, but it was more likely to be a hostile frown. These people had no reason to like them. Quite the contrary.

The guard said something. Kiril felt, almost, that she could understand a little of what he was saying. It was like when she heard a piece of working machinery that after a while began to sound like voices saying something she couldn't quite understand. "What did you say?" she said.

He spoke again, and this time she could make some sense of it, not as words strung together in sentences, but as concepts surfacing that she could understand. If she concentrated hard enough, she could make out his meaning. It was like listening to someone speaking a language she didn't understand fully, but of which she knew just enough words to catch the gist.

What he had said, in essence, was: "Why . . . little ship . . . attack? Dzuna . . . peace."

"Hey, did you hear that?" Kiril said to the others. "We didn't have any luck with their language, but they've been learning ours. A few words, anyway."

They stared at her in puzzlement. "All I heard was their language," said Torwald. He sounded concerned. "You'd better take it easy, Kiril. The hunger may be getting to you."

"But I understood him, plain as anything. A little, anyway."

"Maybe you thought you did," Michelle said doubtfully. "What did you hear him say?"

She told them, leaving in the pauses where she hadn't understood. When she got to the word "Dzuna," she had trouble with it. The alien's vocal equipment wasn't human and the sounds were difficult.

"What does that word mean?" Torwald asked.

"It's what they call themselves," she said. It seemed to be obvious.

"How could you know that?" Nancy asked. "Even if you heard him say human words, you've never heard that one before. Without context, it should just be a meaningless sound to you."

"But that's how he meant it!" she insisted. "I know he did! Look, I'll show you." She faced the guard once more and pointed a finger at herself. "Human," she said.

With a double-jointed contortion the guard indicated himself and said, "Gimlil."

"Didn't sound much like 'Dzuna' to me," Torwald said.

"He thinks we're trading names," she said impatiently. "I'll try again." She pointed at herself: "Human." She pointed at Nancy: "Human." At Torwald: "Human." At Michelle: "Human." She waved to include them all: "Human."

The guard indicated himself, then waved to take in the whole installation. "Dzuna," he said. At least it was close to the word Kiril had repeated. The first sound was a sort of buzz and the *n* sound had the tinge of an *l*, but it was plain enough.

"Well," said Torwald, considerably subdued, "at least now

we know what to call them. That's a help."

"Try to say something to him," Michelle said. "Tell him he's wrong about us."

"Look," Kiril said to the guard, "it wasn't us that attacked you. It was somebody else." The guard's features shifted slightly, but he showed no comprehension.

"Use simple words, Kiril," Nancy advised. "Leave out tenses, use only the present. Use as few words as you can to get meaning across."

Kiril nodded. She waved at her friends and herself and spoke very slowly. "We not attack."

The guard's brow ridges went up and his cheekbones went down, widening his eyes enormously. He had a great deal more facial mobility than his bony features indicated. "We . . . see . . . little ship . . . your ship . . ." She could tell how astonished he was.

Kiril translated for the others. They had heard only gibberish, but there had been no mistaking the violent change of expression the second time Kiril had addressed him. "I'm not surprised he was astonished," Michelle said. "I believe he heard you speaking his language, just as you heard him speaking yours the first time."

"This is getting spooky," Torwald said. "You think she's able to communicate with them telepathically?"

"Do you have a better explanation?" Michelle asked. "She's shown plenty of indications before now, and she knew they were there long before we saw them."

"People with esper sensitivity aren't all that uncommon," Nancy said, "but I've never heard of a case where someone could send and receive actual words and sentences."

"Perhaps it's not actually words Kiril is receiving," Michelle said. "In fact, I think it rather unlikely, since she is communicating with an alien. She may be picking up concepts and then her mind puts them into understandable word form."

"What about their name for themselves, 'Dzuna,'" Torwald said. "She got that."

"She heard that word spoken," Michelle said. "Maybe what she picked up with that word was a concept of racial identification. Homer speculated that the odd pauses in their language might be bridged by telepathic means. It may be that Kiril is our only hope of ever communicating with these people."

"Kiril," Torwald said, "no more talking with them until we've worked out what to say." She nodded.

"First we have to convince them that we don't want war with them, that it was the treachery of one power-crazed maniac," Michelle said.

"They may not even have such a concept," Nancy said.

"Then," said Torwald, "Kiril's going to have to educate them about just what a contrary species we are. Once we have them convinced, or at least half convinced, that we want peace, we have to get them to search for the *Angel*."

"You think that's a good idea?" Kiril said doubtfully.

"It's our only chance. The *Angel*'s never going into space again, with a thruster out. They have to have help, and they sure can't go calling the navy for rescue. And hasn't it occurred to the rest of you that Izquierda's got to get rid of the evidence?"

"You're right," Michelle said. "He can't afford to have *two* Space Angels in existence. His fake ship is undoubtedly wreckage by now, so he has to eliminate the real one."

"How does he explain the fact that there's no bodies to recover from the fake ship?" Nancy asked.

"There'll be bodies," Kiril said. "Remember those mercs I ran into? There were at least a dozen, probably more. Only six went to take the *Angel*."

"Even if they're in no shape to recognize," Michelle protested, "it'd never stand up to a test. Even if all you have is a few skin cells, you can tell race, sex, and age with the most basic analysis."

"Remember," Torwald said, "when you said there was at least one med officer on that navy ship who was taking bribes? Who do you think will be in charge of the navy's autopsy? I have to hand it to Izquierda, he's thorough. He covers all the possibilities and he gets rid of evidence and witnesses as soon as they've served their purpose. I'd sure hate to have him take a personal dislike to me. Look at the position he's put me in, and he hardly even knows I'm alive."

An hour later, the two medics arrived. The guard spoke to them and their faces produced the eye-widening expression. One went away and the other came in, carrying a platter. He said something to them, and the others pointed to Kiril. He repeated the words, and she frowned in concentration. "He says they think we can eat this stuff, but he'll keep an eye on us just in case."

"I suppose that's the best we can hope for at this point," Torwald said. "I guess I'll go first. It's that or die of hunger." He picked up something that looked like a pale root that had been washed and scraped, and bit into it. He chewed awhile, then swallowed with some effort. "About as tasty as a raw potato," he reported, "but I guess it's edible."

Kiril lifted the lid from a small bowl. Inside were a number of fat, writhing grubs. She slammed the lid back down. "I've been hungry before, but I've never been *that* hungry!" The rest of it was roots or what might have been fruits or vegetables. Some was agreeable. Most was too bitter or acid to eat. The grubs were the only food of animal origin, and nothing had been cooked. It was not a satisfying meal but, if there were no long-term effects, it might keep them alive.

When they had finished eating, Michelle took a small locket from a chain around her neck and passed around tracetabs. The tiny tablets contained the trace elements required to keep a human being healthy when eating food raised on alien worlds. Even when local food supplied the carbohydrates, vitamins, and protein necessary to life and health, it rarely had sufficient trace elements. It might take a while, but a human could die from lack of zinc, phosphorus, or any of dozens of other elements required in infinitesimal amounts by the human body as it evolved on Earth. The medic showed interest, and Michelle gave him several tabs, which he carefully placed in a small canister.

The other medic returned. This time he was accompanied by another alien, who wore the coverall and harness of their captors. They could make out nothing that was an indicator of rank, but something in his bearing and the attitude of the other Dzuna suggested that he was a senior officer.

"Careful, now," Torwald cautioned. "I think we're about to be interrogated by the boss." The head alien squatted and stared at them. His lipless mouth turned sharply down at both corners. They had no way of knowing what his expression signified, but it looked forbidding. Kiril sat in front of him, with her friends close beside her.

The alien began to speak. What Kiril heard was:

"I am (incomprehensible) Kantli . . . Dzuna . . . protector force . . ."

"He's saying his name is Kantli, near as I can say it. He said something else, I think it was his rank or position, but it's a concept so alien I couldn't make anything of it. And he's part of a protection force, or maybe this is all protection force, I can't be sure."

"Why you . . . bring war?" She realized that she was able to understand it was a question by a distinct feeling rather than by word order or intonation. There was a quick conference on what her answer should be.

"We do not start war," she said slowly. "Rogue human make attack. Rogue human want war. Blame us. We victims, like you." When she used the word "rogue," she concentrated as hard as she could on the idea of aberration, of villainy, that this human was a criminal and not representative of the rest. Kantli's cheekbones worked sideways, and she knew that this was a gesture of puzzlement.

"We see. . . . little ship attack . . . same little ship . . . peace talk."

"Not same ship! Rogue bring little ship. Like ours, not same! Rogue attack our ship. Our ship crash. Must find ship. We can prove ship not same. You make . . ." She sought the right word to use. ". . . image of ship attack?"

"We have (incomprehensible)."

"I don't know what it is, but it must be some kind of picture or holo or something," Kiril said after she had translated. She turned back to Kantli. "Find ship. Image prove not same. Must find quickly! Rogue destroy! Rogue not want Dzuna or human to know."

"Why rogue . . . want war?" She translated.

"This isn't going to be easy," Torwald said. "It seemed utterly crazy to us; imagine how they'll take it." They conferred and came up with the simplest possible explanation.

"Vengeance, greed, insanity." Apparently Kantli was familiar with all three concepts.

"How rogue . . . vengeance on Dzuna . . . never . . . human before . . ."

"Not Dzuna!" Unconsciously Kiril made a hand gesture she had never performed before. "Rogue want vengeance on our leader. Want for long, long time. Want to make her outcast by blaming war on her. Humans not want war with Dzuna.''

"Why rogue . . . want . . . vengeance . . .?''

"This is going to be difficult,'' Michelle warned, "but if you can get it across right, it could help us look good.''

"Long ago,'' Kiril said, "rogue kill many, many humans. Our leader denounce. Could not prove.''

"Why rogue . . . kill humans?''

"Greed. Insanity.'' Couldn't get much simpler than that, she thought.

Kantli stood and looked down at Kiril. "Send . . . teacher. You . . . learn (incomprehensible). We . . . look . . . ship.'' He turned and left. The medic took up the platter and followed him. Kiril translated his last speech.

"He wants me to learn, well, he used a word that isn't exactly 'language.' It means that and a lot more.''

"Not surprising,'' Torwald said. "I'm wondering, though, why they refer to our negotiations as a 'peace talk,' as if we were settling a war, or avoiding one.''

"Maybe because we showed up with a warship,'' Nancy said.

"Or maybe,'' Torwald said, "these people are so warlike that the first thing they settle when they meet somebody is that there is or isn't going to be a war. Let's hope not.''

"I may not have translated it quite right,'' Kiril said, "but that was the meaning I got.''

"Did that last statement mean he's instituting a search for the *Angel*?'' Nancy asked.

"I'm pretty sure,'' Kiril said.

"For whatever that's worth,'' Torwald said. "He may just be the CO of this little outpost. If I was an officer like that, and I had a whole planet to search for a single ship, I'd have my work cut out for me. By the way, every time we talk about one of these guys, we say 'he.' Actually, we've no way of knowing what gender they are, or even if they have such. We've run across plenty of life forms that don't have our setup.''

"How about that, Kiril?'' Michelle said. "Did you pick up on anything like that?''

Kiril shook her head. "I said 'she' when I mentioned the skipper, but I don't know what he heard.''

"Until we know better,'' Torwald said, "I guess 'he' will

have to remain our pronoun of choice. 'It' makes them seem like nonintelligent creatures, and I hate to think of burly, tough-looking characters who have guns on me as 'she.' Irrational, I admit.''

Kiril was feeling burned out. She was stumbling from one appalling responsibility to another. Everything, not only their immediate future but maybe even the future of humanity, might hinge upon her ability to communicate with the Dzuna.

10

The instructor arrived the next morning. There had been comings and goings during the night. Dzuna on foot had arrived, presumably patrols reporting in. Small craft that hovered on some kind of suspensor field had moved about at night, showing no lights. All of it showed evidence of wartime conditions and discipline.

"I hope this means contact is being kept with the main settlement," Torwald said. "We're sunk unless we can get in touch with their highest authorities."

"How do we know there *are* any higher authorities?" Michelle had asked. "We don't know how devastating Izquierda's attack was. These may be all that's left."

Torwald had mused on that awhile. "Izquierda would have left them some way of getting off-world. This is an outpost. No sense simply blasting them and stranding them here with no way to tell the homeworld who they're supposed to be at war with."

"What's to keep us from taking advantage of that?" Kiril had asked.

"How so?" Torwald queried.

"I mean, not us, but humans in general. Nagamitsu said that they'd left no way for the aliens to find out where Earth or any of the human colonies were, right? What's to keep the TFCS and the Supernova from skinning out of this system? Why not treat this whole business as a fiasco and just leave? There's lots of galaxy left. Humans could just avoid this sector, and we might not run into the Dzuna for another hundred years."

"That's what I'd do if I was Nagamitsu," said Torwald, "but I'll bet Izquierda thought of that, too. Remember the fuss he made when we landed the first day, how he asked Nagamitsu if he was sure that *Angel*'s records were secure? He was going on record that time. He's found some way to get the coordinates to the Dzuna and blame it on the skipper."

"He engineered the *Angel*'s landing in the first place," Nancy said. "We could have come down on the shuttle like everybody else. But he wanted everybody, human and alien, to get a good look at the *Angel*, close up. That way when his ringer came in, everybody would know just what to think."

Now they were taking in the morning sunlight streaming through the doorway. They had just choked down a breakfast of cold vegetation. The medics had not brought back any of the items they had rejected the day before, and had brought some others. They had yet to try anything really palatable, but so far they were suffering no unpleasant effects. Kiril had tried to engage their guards in conversation, but they had all reacted with a negative gesture, holding the hand with fingers down, flicking towards her with the back of the fingertips. This, she figured, was the equivalent of shaking their heads. Apparently they were now under orders not to try to communicate with the humans.

The instructor arrived alone, passing through with only a word or two to the guard on duty. He looked like the others, except for differing paraphernalia attached to his harness. He wore none of the presumed weapons that the soldiers had strapped to their forearms. He looked around at them and began speaking.

"I guess the boss couldn't describe which of us is the sensitive," Torwald said. "That makes us even, I can't tell them apart either." He pointed to Kiril, using the back of his hand.

"I am Teacher Aktla," he said. Kiril was amazed at how clearly this came across. "I will teach you . . . our (language). Must learn . . . quick. There is little time."

She translated for the others. "He's a lot easier to understand than the others."

"Maybe you're improving," Torwald said, "but communicating is probably this guy's specialty."

"Open mouth," Aktla said. Puzzled, she obeyed. He examined the inside of her mouth. The medics had done this as well. "Your . . . structure is different. Never use . . . sound part of (language) properly. Maybe adequately. Start with . . . vocabulary."

He squatted before her and she sat cross-legged facing him. He unclipped a wide, flat instrument from his belt. It was roughly oval and looked like it was made from some organic substance, like most of the artifacts these people had. Along one side was a series of depressions. He placed it on the ground, then grasped the wrist of Kiril's unwounded arm. He placed her palm flat on the instrument and his long fingers danced over the depressions. "Start with nouns," he said.

Shockingly, a vivid image of an alien ship appeared within Kiril's mind, along with an alien word that meant "ship." She jerked her hand back as if it had been burned.

"What is it?" Michelle said. "Are you all right?"

"I'm okay," Kiril said, "just startled. These people have something that makes books and screens and holos look like scratchings in the dirt."

She placed her hand back on the plate. Aktla's cheekbones were working up and down alternately. This she knew to be an expression of amusement. "Not frightened," she said, "just surprised." His fingers moved across the depressions again, and a series of images and sounds came to Kiril. She repeated the sounds as best she could. Many of the sounds were almost impossible for her to enunciate. Nothing was ever repeated, and there was no need to. She found that once a word and object had been flashed into her mind, she could not forget it.

After an hour she took a break and her friends all gave the teaching machine a try. None of them could get more than a vague, fuzzy picture, not even clear enough to get a real idea of what was intended.

The learning session continued rigorously all day. After a basic vocabulary of several hundred nouns came verbs. Most of these were illustrated by Dzuna performing various actions or of objects going through assorted functions. In a few cases she could not understand what the action was, or else the object illustrated was so alien that she could not understand the concept. She told Aktla when this happened, and he tried again with an alternate illustration. Sometimes the question was cleared up, but there were a few that seemed to be impossible to translate.

The sun was almost down when the teacher brought the lesson to a close. "Your (progress?) is good. Tomorrow we try more difficult parts of (speech?) and . . . concepts. By the day after, you must be proficient." He left. Kiril leaned back against the wall of the hut, exhausted. Her brain ached with the new information, and alien words buzzed in her mind. It was too much in too brief a time.

"How's it coming?" Torwald asked.

"I think I'm doing all right," Kiril said, "but the rest of it won't be as easy as today's lesson. Nouns and verbs were easy, both languages have them. But he says there are other things, I guess you'd translate the word he used as 'abstracts,' and I think they're almost purely mental, not spoken. There's other things, too. I don't know if I'm ever going to be able to use their language perfectly, or even well. Maybe I'll be able to get by enough to get us out of this jam, though."

"That's all we ask," Torwald said fervently. "Now, you've been taking in a lot of information. What've you learned about the Dzuna from that instrument?"

"A lot. For instance, you were right when you figured they have a warlike history. I never thought there could be so many words for 'fight.' There's a basic word," she made a gobbling sound, "that just means 'fight.' The image they used was two Dzuna fighting barehanded. Then there was one with two of them fighting with hand weapons, I guess some kind of duel. There were gang fights, then real battles. By the way, those things tied to their arm are weapons, all right. They just make you disappear."

"Disappear?" Michelle said.

"Yes. They point 'em at something and bend their hand down out of the way. No sound and no light, but whatever they point it at just fades away."

"A disintegrator!" Torwald said. "Nobody's ever been able to make one small enough for a man to carry. We've never even developed them as practical weapons. Too much power drain for too little result."

"Let's keep on the good side of these people," Kiril advised. "They're awfully good with those things."

"What about their technology?" Nancy asked. "Did you see any metal, or does it look like they do everything with synthetics?"

Kiril leaned back and closed her eyes. She was as tired as she had ever been. "Not synthetics; organics. They grow everything. They grow their guns and that teaching tool. Their words for 'grow' and 'manufacture' are the same. It all comes out as some kind of agriculture. You want to hear something that's really hard to take? They grow their ships, too." There was a flabbergasted silence.

"That's just not possible," Torwald said.

"Tell them," she advised. "I don't think they'd be very impressed at how we build things. Their way is easy on labor and everything's self-repairing."

"You mean the ships and other objects are still alive after they've reached their final form?" Nancy asked.

"That's the impression I got. Most of them, anyway. The gadget showed a ship-refueling operation in space. It looked like it was happening on a moon or something. The ship just put out roots, like the ones at the bottom of this hut only thicker. They sunk right into the ground and started soaking up chemicals. They use some kind of chemical process to maneuver in-system. I don't know what their interstellar drive is."

"They're not likely to tell us, either," Torwald said. "Not until we can prove we aren't hostile. We probably won't learn how they brake their ships from a free fall to a dead stop, either. It has to be some kind of contragravity force we've never heard of before. Did you figure out—" But Kiril was sound asleep.

* * *

The medic arrived early. This time he had brought some cooked items, including what looked like cubes of dark meat and several shellfish. They had shells, at any rate, and they smelled good. It was far more satisfying than what they had been eating, and they said so. When they had finished eating, the medic reached into a pouch and withdrew something that was flat, hairy, and alive. It pulsed slightly in his hand, then he placed it carefully on the ground.

"Let me . . . see injured arm," he said. Since her lesson the day before, Kiril was having a much easier time understanding him. Hesitantly, she extended her splinted arm. The medic took her arm delicately and extruded a triangular thumbnail perhaps an inch long from his free hand. He ran the nail along the plastic splint, slitting it cleanly. The splint fell away, exposing Kiril's forearm, pale and deeply marked by the ribs of the splint.

The medic picked up the furry thing and wrapped it around her forearm, where it clung tightly. Kiril tensed, expecting pain or itch or some kind of slimy unpleasantness. Instead, the thing spread a pleasant warmth through the arm, and for the first time in days, the throbbing ache subsided and disappeared.

"This will heal you . . . much quicker," the medic said. "We test your . . . systems . . . grow this for right . . . chemistry."

Kiril flexed the fingers of her left hand. They worked better, and the movement did not send shooting pains through her forearm, as it had before. "This is much better," she said.

"Do not try . . . too much," he cautioned. "Pain is gone, but injury is . . . still there."

"I will remember," she said. The medic left and Aktla arrived for the day's language training. Kiril found that the absence of pain in her arm and the satisfaction of a full stomach did wonders for her powers of concentration.

And concentration was what she needed. This day's lessons involved what Aktla had called "abstracts," a word that was difficult to comprehend itself. Many of these were modifiers, expressing radical or delicate shades of nuance through changes in telepathic emphasis. A few of these were fairly simple; differences in emphasis along the lines of "some," "very," "extremely," and so forth. Others were far more complex, and all too many were completely beyond her.

After two hours of intensive work, Kiril sat back, massaging her aching head. "I'll never get good at this," she complained. "Too much of it is just impossible for the human mind to take."

"Don't worry, Kiril," Torwald said. "Nobody expects you to become the Victor Hugo of the Dzuna language. You don't need to do more than get a few basic ideas across to them, like, 'Don't kill us,' and 'Let's call the war off.' And you have to do that convincingly."

"The ideas I can already express," Kiril assured him. "It's getting them to believe me that's going to be hard."

"Do you think they can tell when you're telling the truth?" Michelle asked. "That would simplify things."

"I think maybe they aren't sure," Kiril said. "After all, we're the aliens here. How would they know how to pick up stuff like that? Also, I can pick up some of the telepathic part of their language and understand it, sort of. But am I broadcasting it to them?"

"Ask your teacher," Torwald suggested. That made sense. She asked.

"Poorly," Aktla said. That was a word she had just learned today.

"It's a start," Torwald said with a shrug.

The lesson continued at an ever-increasing pace. As Kiril's powers of comprehension failed her, Aktla piled on the pressure, sending information at an increasing rate. Maybe this helps Dzuna students to learn, she thought, but it's no way to teach a human. Slow and patient is what I need. Nevertheless, Aktla bore on. She found that even when she couldn't understand a concept, it stayed in her mind, anyway.

Aktla broke off abruptly just as the medics returned with their evening meal. "This shall have to . . . do. Perhaps your . . . language skills are now sufficient. In any case, there is no more time. Rest now. We leave tonight." He left without elucidating.

"Leave?" said Torwald when she had translated. "Where to?"

"Did you think he'd tell us?" Kiril asked.

"We never figured they'd keep us in this backwoods base," Nancy said. "Maybe they're taking us in to talk to the top brass."

"I hope so," Torwald said. "They may be rough on us, but we'll do no good until we get to the head people here. The sooner the better."

Kiril was awakened by a gentle nudge in her side. "They've come for us," Nancy said. Kiril sat up, rubbing her eyes. Moving quietly, a small group of Dzuna had assembled before their hut. It was dark outside, but they could tell that some were soldiers, along with the two medics and Aktla.

"Come out." It was the voice of Kantli, the commander. They crawled through the entrance, yawning and stretching. All around them activity was going on, a quiet bustle of Dzuna coming and going. A number of the big antigravity sleds had come in while they had slept, and things were being loaded onto them. A soldier walked up to their hut and fingered a dark patch above the door. There was a rustling sound as the rootlets withdrew from the ground, then a hissing as a mist escaped from the outer walls. The hut began to collapse and shrink.

"They're breaking camp," Torwald said.

"You will come with us," Kantli said. "We leave ahead of the others." Kiril translated this for the other three.

"Do we go now to speak with the Dzuna high command here?" she asked.

"You will have your chance," Aktli answered. "Come."

They followed him to one of the floating rafts and climbed onto it. It was an oval perhaps thirty feet long by fifteen feet in the beam. There was a soft deck surrounded by a low parapet and little else. On other, nearby rafts, they could see loads tied down by hairy vines which grew from the decks. The Dzuna squatted on the deck and the humans sat. Kiril recognized one of the soldiers who squatted near her. "Hello, Gimlil," she said.

"You have been learning to speak like us," he said. She saw that his expression was one of mild surprise. "Your accent is far better than when we first . . . conversed."

"I've done nothing else but study for two days," she aid.

"You have done extremely . . . well for only two days of study. Some . . . aliens never learn at all."

She translated. "So we aren't the first aliens they've run into."

"How did you recognize him?" Nancy asked. "I still can't tell them apart if they're dressed alike."

"I just can," Kiril said. "It's not in the face."

After a brief conference with some other soldiers, Kantli jumped aboard the raft, which shook with his weight. He spoke a few words and a Dzuna squatting in the bow ran his fingers over a control. The raft sped smoothly forward, going under the cover of the trees and easily avoiding the trunks.

On Torwald's instruction, Kiril asked if they were being taken to headquarters.

"There is no central headquarters now," Kantli said. "Since the . . . attack we have dispersed into hidden camps. Now we go someplace . . . else. We will find many of the high command in that place and there will be . . . duties for you to perform."

"Is it to be an interrogation?" she asked.

"Of sorts. We have found your ship and we are taking you there."

The journey went by in a state of nail-biting tension for the four humans. What would they find at the end? Kiril had asked what state the *Angel* was in, but Kantli was either unwilling or unable to tell her. Only Torwald seemed unaffected. He reclined with his back against the parapet and took it easy. He was a man who saw no advantage in worry. What happened would happen, and its effect would not be changed one way or the other by a lot of preliminary hair-tearing. For a change he didn't try to afflict the others with his philosophical musings on the subject.

Light began to stream through the trees, and Kiril woke up. She was surprised to find that she had fallen asleep. The craft swayed from side to side as it sped through the forest beneath the canopy, but so deft was the piloting that the passengers were barely aware of its motion. The craft made no sound she could hear, but there was a faint vibration, almost subliminal. She had been awake only a few minutes when the vibration changed and the raft began to settle to the ground.

The Dzuna soldiers jumped out and trotted purposefully to

various positions surrounding the raft. Then the commander, the medics, and Aktla climbed down. The humans followed. The pilot remained where he was until Kantli said something to him, then he lifted the raft and took it away, back the way they had come.

Torwald scratched and yawned so widely that his jaw made popping noises. "Some things remain the same across the cultures," he observed. "Soon as you land, the foot sloggers set up security, then you send your vehicles off someplace where they can be hidden. They're too easy to see from overhead."

"Why don't they use that masking device?" Nancy asked.

"Good question," Torwald admitted. "We haven't seen a really small one. They had one around their ship, and around the settlement and the camp. Maybe the apparatus is too bulky to use on anything smaller."

The commander was deep in conversation with Aktla. "Kiril," Michelle asked, "can you make out anything they're saying?"

Kiril frowned in concentration. "Almost nothing," she reported. "When one of them is speaking directly to me, it's pretty easy. This way all I get is a few words now and then. I heard the word for 'ship,' and something that means 'supreme chief' or something like that. That's about all."

Kantli came over to them. "From here we walk. The area is . . . secured, full of Dzuna troops. Where we go is within our . . . perimeter, but without overhead cover. We move with proper precautions. Follow."

They went after him, a relatively small group of humans and Dzuna. Nearby but out of sight they could just hear the Dzuna soldiers moving through the brush. As before, the pace was easy. "These Dzuna may not be a hard-marching people," Torwald observed. "Or maybe they're just careful." This time Kantli turned and made a gesture which Kiril told him meant "silence." Torwald shut up.

The ground ascended in a gentle slope, and they crossed a long ridge beyond which was a wide valley. The floor of the valley was a long, flat swamp bristling with grassy hummocks. It was a nesting area for flying creatures, which could be seen wheeling in flocks a few feet above the watery surface. From

time to time a flyer would dive to the water and come up with
something struggling in its mouth. There was a rich odor of
decaying vegetation, not entirely unpleasant. In the northern
end of the valley they could just make out a humped shape on
the swampy floor. It looked as if it didn't belong there.

In the relatively open vegetation of the ridge slope, they
trudged their way north. Nobody said anything. There were
noises nearby that didn't sound as if they were of native origin,
and every so often they would pass the shimmery dome of one
of the Dzuna camouflage fields. As they neared the northern
end of the valley, they could see that a similar field had been
thrown over the humped shape that rose from the marshy floor.

There was a low-voiced exchange in front of them. Aktli was
speaking to someone they could not see. As they passed on,
they saw a pair of sentries crouched behind bushes, their
coveralls blending well into the background. This had to be an
established routine, since precautions like this were of little use
to a force bracing for attack from space. They passed through
the wall of one of the camouflage fields and found a group of
what appeared to be high-rankers. Several of them wore small
jewels set in their harnesses in patterns. One of them was the
dagger-wearing negotiator.

Aktla touched Kiril's shoulder. "This is Supreme Expeditionary Commander Kuth. You will answer all his questions. He
has been told of all you have said so far."

Kuth looked at them without expression. "Come," he said
shortly.

Following him, they passed out of the camouflage field,
crossed a short space of open ground, and went into another,
much larger field. He led them downslope to a last point of high
ground at the edge of the swamp and pointed with the back of
his hand towards the object that already occupied their undi-
vided attention.

A mighty splash in the muddy swamp floor had thrown a
circular wall of mud at least two hundred yards in diameter. The
wall was twenty feet high, but from their point of high ground
they could see into the crater. In its center *Space Angel* lay on
her side, cargo hatch uppermost. From the disposition of the
mud around her, it was clear that she had come in tail first.
Either because of the softness of the ground or the disbalance of

the thrusters, she had been unable to maintain an upright position and had toppled to her side, throwing up another, smaller wall of mud. Both inner and outer crater were slowly filling with water. It was plain that the *Angel* would not be spacing again without help.

Kiril was first to break the long silence. "Is anybody alive in there?"

"First you must answer . . . questions," Kuth said. He squatted on the ground and the other Dzuna did likewise, forming a circle. The humans sat cross-legged and there began the first real human-Dzuna council, with Kiril acting as translator. "You see that we have not . . . harmed the ship. This is not from . . . goodwill but from a . . . desire to learn. You claim that this ship did not . . . attack us. Prove this claim."

"You have an image of the attack," Kiril said. "Show me." Kuth signaled and one of his aides placed a wide plate, much like the teaching machine, before them. Kuth placed his hand on its surface and Kiril followed suit. The effect was far more overwhelming than that of the teaching device. Suddenly she was transported to the landing field where she had spent several tedious days. Only the alien ship was settled there, and she could see the alien colony in the distance. A small group of Dzuna, some in the sort of harness worn by Teacher Aktli, were on the field. They carried instruments and were taking some kind of readings. The time appeared to be early morning.

The image supplied sound as well as sight, for the air was rent by the sound of a ship coming in on thrusters. The team of Dzuna looked up without alarm. The ship that looked like *Space Angel* was coming in. Instead of landing, it hovered about a hundred feet from the ground. Without warning, destructive fire exploded from the ship. From the row of slots around its midriff, sizzling, jagged beams of purple flame slashed out. One struck a settlement building, reducing it instantly to smoking ruin. Another snaked toward the Dzuna ship, but the shimmering field around it had changed. It now reflected light brilliantly from a thousand facets, and the purple beam was reflected away, broken down into a multitude of colored lights.

A beam struck near the small group of Dzuna on the field, then another, smaller-faceted field surrounded the group. The field moved away, toward the treeline, as the researchers fled. Beams from the pseudo-*Angel* continued to slash into the settlement, reducing it to rubble. Nothing seemed to harm the Dzuna ship. The fake *Angel* began to lift, leaving behind a wake of devastation. Just before it was lost to view, something lanced from the Dzuna ship. Then there was silence. Within a minute the Dzuna ship lifted. It accelerated with the same wild disregard it had shown in landing. Within a few seconds it was gone.

Kiril lifted her hand from the plate. Only then did she realize she had been supplying a running commentary to the others. She shook her head. "Can you bring back the image of the attacking ship?" she asked.

Kuth's fingers danced across the plate and Kiril touched it once more. What she saw this time was a frozen scene with no sound. It showed the attacking ship hanging over the field before it had opened fire. Kiril lifted her hand again.

"How many killed?" Michelle asked. Kiril translated.

"No Dzuna died," Kuth said. "Three . . . scientists injured, now healing. No Dzuna in . . . settlement, just in ship and base camps."

"None killed!" Michelle breathed. "We can still salvage something from this."

"You see the row of slots around the middle of the ship?" Kiril asked. "There is no such row of slots on that ship." She pointed to the true *Space Angel*.

"We had noticed," Kuth said. "Is this significant?" Kiril was now running a continuous translation for both sides.

"Our ships are made of metals and synthetics," Torwald said. "Had such slots been cut in our ship, the marks would still be there. Holes in a metal hull will not just heal over."

"Why attack us with weapons so primitive and weak?" Kuth asked.

"What Kiril described to us," Torwald said, "sounds like thrasher beams from a Tesla generator. Obsolete for a hundred years, but just the kind of thing you'd find in a black market arms merchant's inventory. Still used in small wars on small planets. The point was not to destroy you, but to provoke a war. Those big ships in orbit have enough firepower to destroy this planet." Kiril translated as best she could.

"Only if we let you," Kuth said. "Understand, we are quite prepared . . . to fight a war, if that is what you wish. Only because you have indicated that you want peace, that the attack was the work of an . . . aberrant individual, have we hesitated to . . . open hostilities. We thought at first you wanted a contest of strength. This we understand, and it is within our customs. We thought the . . . sneak attack was . . . unsporting, but not without precedent. We do not wish to force a war on . . . unwilling people."

A movement from the ship caught Kiril's eye. "Somebody's alive over there!" she said. Something hauled itself out of the hatch and scuttled along the hull.

"Homer!" Nancy said. "We knew he'd make it. What about the others?"

Another figure climbed from the cargo hatch. It wore a black coverall and walked with a limp. "Finn!" Torwald said with a grin. A third joined the other two. Even at this distance, Lafayette's red hair was plain as a beacon.

"Commander Kuth," Torwald said, "send for one of your rafts. I think it's time you got a close look at our ship and had a talk with our skipper."

The skipper met them at the hatch. After a preliminary round of greeting and back-slapping, she got down to business. "We all made it down in one piece, although a few of us are in the infirmary. Michelle, go take a look at Bert and Achmed. They got banged around a bit." Michelle disappeared below. The skipper turned to Kiril. "So you're our translator, eh? Go to the galley and get some decent food in you. You have a long day's work ahead of you." She turned to Kuth. "Commander, come on in and let's talk."

11

Kiril sipped at a mug of coffee. After the last few days, even coffee tasted good. Besides, she needed the stimulation to keep her overloaded wits from getting groggy. She had spent six straight hours translating, telling her own story, rehashing all the other stories for everybody concerned, and was headed for serious burn-out. Now Homer had taken over. With her key to the language, Homer had learned Dzuna speech at a furious rate. His telepathic talent was slight, but he could discern differences in sound undetectable by the human ear. Once he knew what to listen for, he could supply the ''abstracts'' by tiny differences in tone and volume. It was a relief to have someone else to bear the burden.

Homer had another advantage: Once he had a language down pat, he could translate as each party was speaking. It was like having a translating machine. The moment the words left the speaker's mouth, Homer's translation emerged from whatever alien apparatus served him for vocal equipment.

It looked as if the Dzuna were finally convinced of their

story. "Now, Commander Kuth," the skipper said, "I think it's time you had a look into our computer files. They'll give you a better picture of what happened and a general picture of what we're like."

"Computer?" Kuth said. The word had been translated literally. "A device for adding up numbers?"

"That's how they started out," Torwald said. "The earliest computers were just adding machines. Now they can do most things humans do and some things we can't, like play solitaire without cheating."

"Don't be facetious, Tor," Michelle said.

The skipper got up from her galley chair and led the Dzuna up to the bridge, with Homer scuttling after. Kiril slumped in her chair. When would all this end? Michelle shoved a tray in front of her. Heavenly as it smelled, she barely had the energy to eat.

"Eat that," Michelle ordered. "Then go back to your cabin and sleep. I don't know what's going to be planned, but the way things have been happening, it'll be strenuous."

Kiril nodded tiredly. With relief, she pushed the mug of coffee away. If she was going to sleep, she didn't need to force herself to drink it. Without tasting anything, she cleaned the tray, got up, and began staggering back towards her cabin. There was a lot of clutter and disorder, but the ship didn't look as bad as she had feared. The artificial gravity field had saved the interior from the worst of the fall, and Achmed had managed to dump most of the leaked fuel, but there was some wreckage strewn about. The external damage had been worse. Beside the thruster problems, the hull had been strained and ripped in a dozen places. On a ship as old as the *Angel*, that meant that she would never space again without some time in dock. Docking facilities were in short supply hereabout.

She crossed the hold, where she could clearly see many of the dents and rips in the fabric of the ship. Past the hold she came to the Vivers' quarters. The Vivers were keeping discreetly out of sight. They tended to make people uneasy and might look out of place when the skipper was trying to convince the Dzuna of their peaceful intentions. She stuck her head into the anteroom. "K'Stin?"

The huge Viver appeared in the other doorway. "How does it go?" he asked.

"Slow. Is B'Shant all right?" By way of answer, B'Shant appeared from inside the inner cabin. His carapace was brilliantly shiny and he was now only two or three inches shorter than K'Stin.

"My younger kinsman is now back in fighting shape," K'Stin said. "Tell the skipper that we are now ready to wreak vengeance upon Izquierda and all his works. Besides her own grudge and the fact that he has threatened us all, he has committed yet a greater evil."

"What's that?" she asked.

"He insulted me, B'Shant, and the glorious Clan T'Chak by sending such inferior persons to kill us. I take that personally. Tell her to simply get us aboard the Supernova, preferably armed with heavy-duty beamers. We will do the rest. Perhaps we can break the record for a two-Viver team trashing a major ship."

"I'll pass the word, K'Stin," she said, "but I wouldn't count on her going along with it."

"I speak no disloyalty," K'Stin said, "but the skipper lacks a sense of personal style. It is not enough that these things be done efficiently. Artistry is also necessary."

She pulled her head out and walked the short distance back to her cabin. She knew she should visit Achmed in the infirmary, but she was just too tired. She'd already seen Bert. He was taking things easy in his cabin. She'd see Achmed when she woke up. She locked her hatch behind her. Teddy was asleep on her bunk and she lifted him off. She collapsed into the bunk and was asleep somewhere between starting her fall and hitting the mattress.

Something felt different when she woke up. The chrono display on the bulkhead told her that she had slept for twelve hours. She pushed herself to a sitting position and then realized that she had used her left arm to do the pushing. That was what was different. She looked at the arm. The furry "splint" was gone. Her arm showed no sign of injury. She flexed her fingers. They worked perfectly and there was no pain. She searched her bunk for the splint. Finally she found it on the deck beneath her bunk. It had shrunk like a withered leaf, with nothing left but a paper-thin membrane with a fuzzy surface.

Kiril splashed some water in her face and decided she would live. In fact, she felt fine, better than she had since this whole business had started. Either a good meal and a night's sleep had great recuperative qualities or the alien whatzit did more than fix broken bones. Whatever happened next, she felt up to facing it. Within limits, of course.

On her way to find out what was happening, she stopped by the infirmary. She found Achmed alone, apparently asleep. He had been burned and had a number of impact injuries. He was nearly covered with the furry things. Michelle must have persuaded the Dzuna medics to give her some help.

The skipper glanced up as Kiril entered the mess room. "You're looking better," she said. Her eyes were red-ringed and she slumped in her chair with fatigue. It looked as if negotiations had been going on while Kiril slept.

"I feel fine." She took a chair. "Where are the Dzuna and the rest of the crew?"

"The Dzuna left about an hour ago. Everybody else is asleep. Draw me some coffee, will you?"

Kiril got up and went into the galley. As she drew the skipper's cup, she noticed a note clipped to a cabinet. Michelle had made out a menu for her and reminded her sternly to take another tracetab. She got a beaker of her concentrated nutrient from a refrigerator and went back into the mess room.

"The upshot of our talks with the Dzuna," the skipper began, "is that they're willing to enter peaceful trade negotiations. That would be of great benefit to both races. Their command of biochemistry and biomechanics boggles the mind. In turn, they're fascinated by our metallurgy and computer technology. Their equivalent instruments are bulky and inefficient by comparison. That's just for beginners. All that's standing in the way is Izquierda."

"What can we do about that?" Kiril asked. She drank from the beaker and made a face. She was getting sick of the stuff.

"We have to prove that the *Angel* had no part in the attack, and we have to be convincing."

"That won't be hard, if we can just get to the navy ship," Kiril said. "Just being alive proves something. By now Izquierda has faked the destruction of the *Angel* with all aboard. If we can just get them to train instruments on this swamp, they'll see that the *Angel* wasn't destroyed. Can we beam a signal? We sure can't fly up there and talk to them. This ship's going nowhere for a while."

"I proposed much the same to Kuth. This planet's under tight military security. They're afraid that any signal like that could breach their security. I'd do the same in their place. We can't ask that of them."

"That's no help," Kiril said. "Did the Dzuna have any suggestions?"

"One. They can put a small ship at our disposal. It's *very* small, smaller than that raider you arrived in. But it has their masking device. All their information says none of our sensors can penetrate that masking. They can send up two or three of us. If we can get aboard one of those ships, we can give Nagamitsu the coordinates for the *Angel*. Then whoever boards the ship can beam down a signal and the Dzuna will drop the masking of this ship for a few minutes. They'll have cleared out of the area, so the only danger is that Izquierda will catch the coordinates and try to heave a bomb in on us."

"Do you think any of us could get aboard the TFCS?"

The skipper shook her head. "Not a chance. Even if that little ship can get close enough without being detected, a TFCS on full wartime alert is the most heavily defended object in space. There's no way in once it's buttoned up." She set her coffee cup down carefully. "It's got to be the Supernova. It has nothing like the defenses of the TFCS, and we know that Izquierda has one hold and hatch that he keeps out of sight from the navy ship. The one he launched the fake *Angel* from."

"Who goes?" Kiril said, with a sinking feeling.

"I'm not putting this to a vote," the skipper said, "because I'd have a mutiny on my hands. I want you to go. You have the right to refuse, of course. But you know the inside of that ship. Most of all, you're the one who heard it all from Izquierda first hand. Even if he destroys the *Angel* and kills the rest of us, your story will stand up to government interrogation."

Suddenly Kiril felt weak. To go back aboard that ship again!

Nothing in space or on the alien planet was as frightening as being within Izquierda's power again. She thought about what was at stake, for a long time. "All right," she said shakily, "I'll go."

The skipper sat back in her chair. "I know what that cost you. Tor told me what you asked him to do. Who'll you take with you?"

"The Vivers," she said without hesitation. "Give them beamers, they're itching to restore their honor."

For the first time the skipper cracked a faint smile. "Good choice, but I can't let them have beamers. I'll admit I was never so shocked in my life as when you told me Izquierda had unsecured beamers aboard ship." She shook her head. "It's hard to believe a ship's officer could act like that. Don't worry, those two can raise plenty of hell without beamers."

"When do we go?" Kiril asked, now anxious to get it over with, one way or the other.

"It'll take them maybe a day or two to bring the ship here masked." The skipper lit up one of her noxious cigars and turned, if anything, even more serious. "Look, Kiril, I realize I have no business even talking about the future, since there's not much chance any of us have one, but I want to say a few things. You know that the ship's kid usually has to leave when he or she outgrows the job?"

"I've been told."

"We never just beach them. When they leave the *Angel*, they have an apprentice spacer's bracelet and we always make sure they have a berth before they leave. But there've been exceptions. Lafayette was one."

"He told me about that." Was this what she hoped it was?

"I want you to be another. I want you to stay with the *Angel*. You can apprentice for any position on the ship, except for engineer, which goes to Lafayette." The skipper crossed her arms on the table and leaned forward. "I mean this, Kiril. If it's my job you'd like, I'll see to it you have your chance. I can't live forever. If you want a bridge officer's position, just say the word. It'd mean a few years away from the ship at one of the academies, but I'd pay for the schooling."

Kiril turned away quickly, her eyes stinging. "Let me think about it."

"Sure," said the skipper. "There's lots of time. Pretty soon there may be no ship, anyway. I just wanted you to know. You always have a place with us. Understood? That's already sworn into the ship's log, with Ham as witness, just in case I don't make it but you and the *Angel* do."

"I understand," Kiril said. There was absolutely nothing else she could think of to say.

"Now get yourself something solid to eat and rest up. I've got work on the bridge. Don't talk about your mission to anyone except K'Stin." The Skipper left, and Kiril was alone with her thoughts. The distant future, with her as a permanent resident aboard the *Space Angel*, she pushed from her mind. It was the immediate future that concerned her.

She ate hastily and went to the Vivers' compartment. So far she had seen none of the others. She rapped on the hatch of the inner room and it snapped open with startling swiftness. "What is it, small and skinny one?" K'Stin demanded. "Is it danger?"

"Not now, but soon. We have to talk in private." She stepped inside and K'Stin closed the hatch. In the tiny room she could hardly 'turn around without bumping into one of the Vivers. Before, the hulking, armored creatures had always made her nervous. After Izquierda, though, nothing seemed very scary.

"We're going to go hit the Supernova," she said. "Just me and the two of you."

K'Stin's rigid face could not grin but it was in his voice. "Fun at last. When do we go?" She told him of the skipper's plan. "Will we take beamers?"

"She says no. It's against the rules."

"Foolishness!" K'Stin groused. "We Vivers are not mere pulpy humans with no sense of space and distance."

"I thought you *were* humans," she said, "just gene-manipulated."

"True, but we don't like to think about it. We have the most perfect of distance perception and orientation. I could set the beam-length control to sweep a hold without cutting the paint on the far bulkhead."

"Relax, K'Stin. She's not letting you take any beamers from here aboard the Supernova, but we're going in through the hold where the mercs have their quarters. I know where the weapon racks are. I, for one, am not worried about breathing vacuum. Not with Izquierda to think about.''

The Viver enveloped her shoulder in his huge hand. ''You have the proper spirit, skinny one. You should have been a Viver.''

She felt a little better when she left the Viver quarters. If she had to go in with somebody at her back, the Vivers were the best possible choice. She wondered what to do. The skipper had told her to rest up for her mission, but she felt fully rested and energized. Better, in fact, than she had felt in years. Then she saw all the litter that was still lying about from the crash and she remembered that she was still ship's girl and had a job to do.

For the next few hours Kiril swept and picked up, loading the wreckage into a wheeled hauling cart to be tossed into the ship's trash compacter. Anything that was too heavy for her to pick up, she left until one of the men could give her a hand. When she had the main corridor straightened away, she worked on the mess room and galley. There wasn't all that much to do there, because the rest of the crew had already done most of it. She went to her own cabin and tidied it up and then wondered what else she could do to keep herself from thinking about what was ahead.

Michelle found Kiril mopping up in hydroponics and scolded her for overexerting herself. Kiril said that she felt fine, and Michelle left. A few minutes later Lafayette appeared and took the mop. Gently but firmly he shoved her into the corridor and told her to go relax. The rest of the day went like that. She wished she could tell Michelle to leave her alone. The medic's determination to look out for Kiril's health was having the opposite effect.

After the evening meal she went to her cabin and stretched out on her bunk. She fidgeted and fretted but could not sleep. It was an unusual experience. In the past she had slept under the rubble of half-collapsed buildings, on the lumpy floors of cellars, in the chilling cold of rain-swept doorways. All she'd had to do was close her eyes to nod off, always ready to waken instantly at the approach of danger. Now she couldn't sleep, in comfort and relative safety. Even in the Supernova she'd slept.

She remembered the soporific that had lulled her in the big ship. Maybe that was what she needed.

She got up and dressed, then went to Michelle's quarters. She found the medic writing something on a glowing screen with a stylus. "I can't sleep," Kiril told her. "You got anything that'll put me out?"

Michelle dropped the stylus to her desk and glared accusingly at Kiril. "She's sending you back up there again, isn't she? To the Supernova."

"I thought you weren't telepathic," Kiril said, shocked by the sudden anger.

"Who needs it?" Michelle said. "I've been watching you all day. You've always been attentive to your duties, but after all we've been through, anyone would kick back for at least a day. You've been working like you just got the job and you think you'll be fired if someone sees you taking a break. You're terrified, aren't you?"

"The skipper told me not to talk about it."

"You might as well, or I'll go up to the bridge and have it out of her. Now talk."

Reluctantly Kiril unfolded the story. Michelle listened with a stony expression. "It's crazy."

"It's the only way and you know it," Kiril said. "I'm not happy about it, but I'm ready to go through with it. It's what the Dzuna will go along with, and we need their ship."

"But it doesn't need to be you," Michelle protested. "You've already done more than ever should have been asked of you. Do you have any idea how the rest of us have felt, knowing that you've been taking all the risks?" Kiril was speechless, seeing the tears standing in Michelle's eyes. "You should have seen this crew that second night you went aboard that ship. Ham and Finn and Torwald snarled and snapped at one another like dogs that don't like each other's scent. Lafayette sulked in the engine room and wouldn't come out to eat. Bert wouldn't answer the skipper when she talked to him, and Nancy spent the whole night in the observation bubble, playing her violin. Achmed prayed all the time. Even the Vivers were more insufferable than usual."

"And you?" Kiril asked quietly.

"I told her if anything happened to you, she could transfer me to the TFCS. I'd get a position as a hospital assistant until we reached port and I could find another ship."

"You mean this crew was breaking up over *me*?" Kiril said, incredulous. "Why? I wasn't taking any more risk than the rest. We were all under death sentence the minute we got that summons. Izquierda's been planning to destroy this ship and everyone in it for years! Unless we can find a way out of this jam, none of us are gonna live. What difference does it make if I get it aboard that ship or in this one?"

"At least it wouldn't be *him*!" Michelle said, vehemently. "Nobody should be asked to put himself into that man's power, and you've done it twice, realizing what he was even before the rest of us did, and now you're going to do it again. It's not fair."

"Fair?" Kiril said. "I've heard gamblers use that word, but they all cheat. It doesn't apply here. We got to do what we can to get us out of this, and I'm in a position to do us some good. The skipper's plan is sound. She's got the whole ship to think about. I'm the one who can testify about Izquierda, and if anybody can keep me alive long enough to do it, it's those Vivers. Besides, I think I have one other advantage."

"What's that?" Michelle asked, dabbing at her eyes.

"Remember what I said a while back, about how Nagamitsu hates Izquierda's guts, even worse than the skipper?"

"Yes. What of it? Probably most of the navy officers who've heard what he did during the War hate him."

"It's more than that. He has some other reason and it's personal. I think all he needs is an excuse to move against Izquierda. Well, I can give him that excuse. I don't think he'll waste any time."

"Are you sure?" Michelle asked.

"I've been right about these things so far, haven't I?"

Michelle slumped with her face buried in her palms, and Kiril stepped behind her and put her hands on the older woman's shoulders. After a few minutes Michelle rummaged through a drawer and handed Kiril a small packet of tabs. "Here. It could happen tomorrow, and you'll need some sleep. Take one of these."

Kiril took them and went back to her cabin, not trusting herself to say anything more. She was glad that the tab was fast-acting, because it was the first time she had ever cried herself to sleep since she was a little girl.

"The two ships," Kuth was saying, "are in orbit around the great moon. We suspect that is because . . . they can make a faster . . . getaway should things turn bad. It is only . . . prudent. One of our vessels picked up a piece of wreckage in planetary orbit. It contained the . . . memories of one of your computers. Among them was . . . location data of many human worlds. The . . . chances of making such a find are unthinkable. This was the work of your . . . traitor."

"We expected such a move," the skipper said. "The instruments will prove to be from the fake *Angel*. Another nail in our coffin. The man overlooks nothing. As long as you don't attack the ships, they won't leave or attack you. They're trying to figure out a way to patch up this situation while Izquierda plumps for war. He must want to get out bad by now. He doesn't want hostilities to commence while he and his ship are vulnerable."

"What's stopping him?" Torwald asked.

"Nagamitsu," she answered. They were gathered around the mess table once again. "He must suspect Izquierda had something to do with all this. He's making him keep the Supernova close to the TFCS. Old Ramon must be sweating about now."

Kiril had arrived a few minutes before. She ate silently while the skipper and the Dzuna commander talked. Would today be the day? She was scared and unhappy, but she was ready to go through with it. She found that it wasn't easy to swallow, and she was afraid that people would notice, so she sat back, ignored her plate, and confined herself to sipping tea.

Most of the crew had wandered in, still yawning and stretching. They were dozily drinking coffee when Kuth broke off what he was saying and ran his fingers over a plate strapped to his forearm. "The ship is here," he announced through Homer. "It is time."

The skipper's eyes locked with Kiril's for a long second.

"Let's go." Afterwards, Kiril wasn't sure which of them had said it. She got up and noticed Michelle, sitting stone-faced, looking at nothing.

Slow on the uptake, Torwald looked around in puzzlement. "Ship? What the hell is—" But Kiril and the skipper were already following Kuth out of the mess room.

"K'Stin, B'Shant," the skipper called. The two Vivers fell in behind them, blocking the corridor as the rest came pouring out of the galley area, shouting and asking questions.

They came out into the airlock room, where the Vivers picked up the weapon harnesses they had waiting there. "What is this?" Finn shouted. "Hold it! Where are you sending her?"

"Where do you think?" Torwald said. "She's going back up to the Supernova. Why else send the Vivers? Skipper, you can't send that kid back up there, it's certain death!"

"There's no choice," said the skipper. "We have to prevent a war. Maybe she can stop it. It's a chance."

"But it doesn't have to be her!" Torwald protested. "Send me. Send any of us!"

"She has the best chance," said the skipper.

"But we didn't vote on this," Lafayette said.

"This isn't a democracy," said the skipper. "In a matter of this importance, all responsibility rests with me as captain. I say she goes."

"She does not go alone this time," K'Stin said.

"Even you and B'Shant aren't that good," Finn said.

A Dzuna raft floated to the hatch. "Get in," the skipper said. Torwald, Finn, and Lafayette surged forward. With a back-handed sweep of his arm B'Shant sent the three big men tumbling like dolls to crash into a bulkhead. Ham watched impassively. "You're outclassed, men," said the mate.

"K'Stin," Torwald said. The bigger Viver turned to face him. "If anything happens to Kiril, make sure it happens to you, too. If she doesn't come back, don't you come back, either."

K'Stin made a sound that might have been a laugh. "I choose not to be insulted. If we cannot stop war, we will at least have revenge. We will bring her back unharmed or we will die gloriously. Izquierda and his proud ship will not return to savor the fruits of treachery. If we die, let all know what happens to any who would threaten the Vivers or any under their protection." He shrugged into the weapon-studded harness and climbed onto the raft.

The raft pulled smoothly away from the ship. Kiril avoided looking back. "Skipper," she said, "I think maybe you better not go back there for a while."

The skipper snorted a cloud of cigar smoke. "They'll cool down. They know it had to be done, they just don't like it, that's all. It's part of being skipper, Kiril. You try to be too popular and you start making the wrong decisions. You start trying to keep people happy instead of doing what's best for the ship."

"I know," Kiril said. She sat cross-legged with her arms wrapped around herself. Her stomach felt as if tied in a knot. She doubled over with a spasm of agonizing nausea and clenched her teeth so tightly together that her jaw hurt.

"You okay?" the skipper said. She gripped Kiril's shoulder.

Kiril straightened up. As the spasm passed, the numbing terror dropped away. The fear was still there, but she was used to fear. She had lived with it all her life. "I'm okay," she said, and she meant it. The worst was over. Now that things had at last started, she felt much better. She knew that she would do her best without letting the fear get in the way.

"Here's your signaler," the skipper said. She handed Kiril a flat box with a belt clip. It was the size of Kiril's hand and had a single, square pressure plate in its middle. "I spent half the night cobbling that together. As soon as you have Nagamitsu's attention, hit that plate. It'll send out two signals simultaneously. One to the instruments on the TFCS, pinpointing the location of the *Angel*. The other to the *Angel* herself. When I get that signal, I tell Kuth and he drops the camouflage field. Then Nagamitsu may just have a few minutes to act. Izquierda's people on the TFCS are sure to tell him what's happened, and he'll be frantic to destroy the *Angel*, both to get rid of the evidence and as a last chance for revenge."

"You'll evacuate the ship, won't you?" Kiril said. "I mean, there's no sense being there when a bomb hits."

The skipper shrugged. "Any that want to leave can do it."

The raft entered a masking field in a narrow valley. They saw a near-spherical blob with a smooth surface, anchored to the ground by what appeared to be hairy cables. As the raft settled near the sphere, they could see that the "cables" were roots growing from the sides of the thing. There was a gaping hole in the side of the sphere, and it had no visible door or other closure.

"Looks like this is where I leave you," the skipper said. They dismounted and the Vivers looked at the sphere suspiciously.

"This is a ship?" K'Stin said. "It looks like a tumorous growth on a beebleberry plant. Can Vivers commit themselves to so unseemly and ignoble a craft?"

"You must prevent a war," the skipper said. "If war comes to human space, that's Viver space, too. The Dzuna would be an unknown enemy, and the whole Viver race would be endangered."

"That is true," K'Stin said. "There comes a time when individual safety and dignity must be sacrificed for the good of Clan and People." He and B'Shant ducked inside, their harnesses aclatter with swords, daggers, and other lethal hardware.

"That's one good thing about Vivers," the skipper muttered, "their psychology is comparatively simple and straightforward."

"This is . . . pilot Sholk," Kuth said. "He will give you your . . . instructions. Now perform your task." The Dzuna leader turned and walked away.

"He didn't even wish us good luck," Kiril said.

"Maybe he doesn't know how," surmised the skipper. "Anyway, I'll say it. Good luck, Kiril."

"Same to you," Kiril said hastily. She took a deep breath and went inside, followed by the pilot. He looked like all the others, but his harness was bright blue. Kiril turned to see the skipper waving good-bye as the opening grew shut from the edges. A dim light seeped through the sides of the craft.

The pilot faced Kiril. "Sit on the . . . floor. This is an . . . escape and rescue craft, not intended for . . . conventional space flight. It will not be a . . . comfortable journey. When we near the nonmilitary ship, you must direct me to the correct dock."

"How?" Kiril said. "I can't see out of this thing."

"When the time comes, you will . . . see as I see."

"I can point out the right dock," Kiril said, "but I can't open it."

"I will take care of that," the pilot said. "Now sit."

Kiril sat on the soft, springy deck and the Vivers did likewise. Abruptly vines sprung from the walls and wrapped themselves around Kiril and the two Vivers. Even the massive strength of the Vivers was futile against them. "Treachery!" shouted K'Stin, struggling against the vines.

"Easy, K'Stin," Kiril said. "They're just takeoff restraints." She jerked her head towards the pilot. He was likewise restrained where he squatted before a large bump of protoplasm that bulged from one wall. Only his arms were free, and he sunk his fingers into the blob. A pulsing began, accompanied by an almost-subliminal heartbeat rhythm. Far more than the big Dzuna ship they had seen, or the skimming rafts, this craft resembled a living thing. The walls were ribbed with struts or veins and every surface in sight was some kind of living tissue. It was unsettling.

"I feel like I've been swallowed by something," Kiril said.

"Don't talk like that," K'Stin cautioned.

The pilot said something, but Kiril couldn't quite make it out since he was not facing her. The ship took off with such violence that Kiril lost consciousness within seconds. When she woke up, it was dark and she could taste blood in her mouth. In the dimness she could just make out the Vivers, now floating in freefall, with only a single vine holding each.

"How long have I been out?"

"Only a few minutes. The shock did not affect us. These Dzuna are able to withstand G-forces much better than ordinary humans."

"No kidding." She took a kerchief from her pocket and wiped away the blood that had been streaming from her nose. In freefall it had collected into a single blob stuck to her upper lip. "I guess since this is an escape ship, they don't want it to waste any time. I wonder if we can scare up some light?"

K'Stin took a cube from his belt and it began to glow, slowly growing brighter, giving her eyes time to adjust. The pilot paid no attention. "The flight should be short," K'Stin said. "That was a long acceleration. We have been in freefall for only a minute or two. We must discuss our plans. As soon as we are inside the lock, you must show us where the weapons are stored.''

"Sure,'' she said. "If they're still there. Izquierda may have cleared out all evidence of his plan by now.''

"We will try,'' K'Stin said. "We will be at the rear of the ship. You must get forward, to the communication equipment. We will clear a path for you.''

"I don't think you should do that,'' Kiril said. "I think you should be raising hell in some other part of the ship while I make my own way forward. With you, I'll be meeting resistance all the way. But who's going to notice me with all the alarms going off?''

"That is tactically sound,'' K'Stin admitted, "but I do not want to let you out of my sight. I am charged with protecting you, as well as with stopping Izquierda.''

"Come on, K'Stin, what's more important, my life or stopping this thing? Don't get all sentimental on me. The whole crew's been acting like I was their delicate little kid sister who needs to be protected. I was as good as dead when Tor found me. I've had a few good months that're pure bonus time since then. If I go, nobody's lost anything, including me. Now let's go destroy that cancer on the body of humanity, and let's do it my way and cut out all this nonsense.''

K'Stin said nothing for a few seconds, then: "We do it your way. You have the soul of a Viver, skinny one.''

12

"Come here," the pilot said. They were still decelerating, and there was enough false gravity for Kiril to walk over to the pilot. The vines had dropped away from them when the deceleration had begun an hour before. They had been in flight for about six hours. "Touch the . . . (?)"

There was no translation, but she knew that he meant the bulge of tissue into which his own fingers were sunk. Cautiously she extended her own hands. The stuff was warm and it pulsed faintly. Her fingertips sank into it, an odd but not unpleasant experience. Abruptly she was drifting in a black void, her brain responding directly to the visual receptors of the living "ship." Before them was the vast form of the Supernova. A few kilometers beyond it she could see the TFCS. Whatever masking processes the ships were employing, they were ineffective, at least at this range.

"Where is the hatch?" the pilot said. She heard him clearly, even though her real ears could not respond in this trance state. The window in her mind, the one through which she alone of the human team had been able to communicate, was fully open.

"Port side. The line of oval hatches beginning amidships. The second from the stern."

"Is the hold mostly forward or aft of the hatch?"

"The hatch is dead center."

"Where is the deck?"

"The bottom of the hatch is flush with the deck."

"That is all I need to know. You may withdraw. Contact in three minutes. Entry a few seconds after that."

Kiril pulled her fingers loose and shook her head. "Get ready. We'll be in there in about three minutes."

K'Stin took a bag from his harness and withdrew a half-dozen plastic balls the size of Kiril's fist. He hung these from his harness and passed the bag to B'Shant, who took the rest of the balls.

"What're those?" Kiril asked suspiciously.

"Grenades," K'Stin said.

"I thought the skipper kept those things locked up."

"She did. But Ham is a thoughtful and sensible being who does not share her prejudice against damaging ships' hulls when extreme circumstances call for it."

"Yeah, he's a treasure, all right," she said, remembering the little dagger that might have saved them all.

A bump went through the little ship and they were in freefall again. One side of the vessel began to flatten, as if it were pressing against some solid surface. A tiny hole appeared in the center of the flattened area. It widened, exposing an expanse of shiny metal. "That's the side of the Supernova!" Kiril said.

A series of small holes opened in the fabric of the Dzuna craft surrounding the opening. There was a sizzling sound. "Acid!" K'Stin said. Fumes began to come from the edges of the exposed metal, and they were sucked up by the surrounding holes. Within ten seconds the metal fell inward, exposing the brilliantly lit interior of the hold.

"In quickly!" K'Stin shouted, "before the self-sealer gets to work." He kicked himself away from a wall and shot through the opening, quickly followed by B'Shant. The two did a flip in midair and landed on their feet within the Supernova's gravity field. Kiril followed more cautiously. Even so, she stumbled when she crossed the threshold from freefall to gravity.

"Where are the weapons?" K'Stin demanded. Sirens were shrieking throughout the ship and emergency signals flashed in the hold. Behind them the self-sealer oozed from the edges of the hole, hardening as it expanded inward. Within five seconds the breach was sealed.

Kiril scanned the hold. It looked different and much bigger without the ship in it. She spotted a walkway a little above deck level. A row of four doors opened onto the walkway. She pointed. "There! Second door from the left."

The two Vivers covered the distance in a blur. The door on the far right opened and a white-clad merc appeared through it, trying to decide between pulling on a pressure helmet and drawing a pistol. B'Shant's arm flexed casually and a grenade sailed through the door behind the man. There was an eruption of flame and smoke and more alarms began yammering. The Vivers easily leaped the barrier between the deck and the walkway. B'Shant ripped the door open, nearly unhinging it, and K'Stin charged inside with a short, broad-bladed sword in his fist. B'Shant followed instantly.

Kiril ran across the huge deck as shouts and sounds of battle came from within the room. By the time she reached the walkway, the two Vivers were back out on the deck. Each had a pair of pistols on their belts and a heavy-duty beamer in each hand. Their harnesses were crammed with small objects of various sizes. "What are those?" Kiril asked, pointing to the plates, cylinders, sticks, and other things.

"Explosives," K'Stin said. "Now, show us where we want to go."

"This way." She dashed onto the walkway and took the first door. It led into a passage ending at the corridor where she had first encountered the merc. It seemed like a long time ago. She waved them back and eased the door open. The corridor was empty, but the din from alarms and the flashing signs made it raucous. "Okay, let's go, and don't go around just killing people."

"We want Izquierda," K'Stin said. "And we want to trash this ship. We attack only those who shoot at us. The mercs are fair game."

"Agreed," Kiril said. She darted out and began to run

forward. K'Stin darted around her and B'Shant fell in behind. She found the lift and they crowded inside. As it began to drop, B'Shant heaved a packet of sticks back the way they had come. His throw was so powerful that the packet just skimmed the ceiling and then bounced along the deck until it almost reached the bulkhead between the hold area and the engine section. They were just below the level of the deck when they heard the shattering explosion. The Vivers shook and made chuckling sounds all the way down.

They became businesslike as soon as they were out of the lift. K'Stin fired his left-hand beamer, holding the big shoulder weapon at arm's length as if it had been no more than a pistol. He cut away a bulkhead, shearing through power lines, communication optic fibers, fuel pipes, and chemical conduits. Empty rooms beyond became visible, and he cut away portions of them, not pausing in his leisurely walk down the corridor. B'Shant did the same on the opposite side. Kiril could see that they were slicing away nearly everything between them and the outer skin of the ship. The air filled with a chemical reek and smoke began to billow, choking the ventilation systems. Fire-fighting systems cut in, spraying water and fire suppressants in all directions.

Kiril watched in wonderment as the two methodically dismantled the entire level of the Supernova. True to K'Stin's promise, the beams never quite reached the outer skin. From time to time one would toss an explosive at some supporting structure. The structure would be blown away and the deck above would begin to sag in. The Vivers each slung one heavy-duty beamer and drew a pistol. With quick, efficient shots, they knocked out sensors with one hand while they continued demolition operations with the other.

"There's people up there!" Kiril said. She was beginning to get choked up from the smoke and fumes. Inflatable emergency escape pods were bursting from the walls and respirators dropped from traps in the overhead. She grabbed a respirator and strapped it around her face.

They burst into a chamber full of construction workers. The workers were scrambling into escape pods, yanking on pressure suits and respirators, clearly expecting an abandon-ship order. It was understandable, since the cacophony of alarms sounded like the end of the universe.

"Calm yourselves!" K'Stin bellowed. "You will not be harmed as long as you do not resist."

"Listen to him!" Kiril yelled, her voice muffled by the respirator. "Satsuma won't pay any bonuses or pensions if you die defending this ship. Just relax, get into the pods if it makes you feel safer. These two mean business!" The workers gaped at them. This was something outside the experience of even the combat veterans.

Nobody tried to slow them down as they passed through the housing area. Demolitions commenced once again on the other side. They continued in this fashion, bypassing occupied areas, turning everything else into a junkheap. It seemed to take a long time, but Kiril glanced at her watch and saw that they had been inside the Supernova only a few minutes.

The Vivers really hit their stride when they reached the mall area. There were no workers present, and they slashed in all directions with apparent abandon but using incredible precision. Each cut and explosion took out some crucial structural member, toppling structures and undercutting the support of the levels above. Within three minutes the mall level above began falling into the one they occupied.

"You gotta leave me a way up to the bridge!" Kiril yelled.

"We have not cut the lift," K'Stin said, not pausing in his work. "Its power supply is independent of the others, since it is an escape necessity. Go on up, we will give you a few minutes, then we come looking for you."

Kiril darted into the lift and hit the plate for the command level. From above the destruction wrought by the Vivers was even more appalling. The next level was nearly as devastated, with its supports cut away. Gaping holes had appeared in the deck and buildings sagged. She got off on the command level, which was full of people running and shouting. Most of them had pressure suits on, and as she had expected, nobody paid her the slightest attention.

A voice was calling in an incongruously calm voice over the comm system: "*Please do not panic. The hull is intact. The interior damage is being contained. I repeat, please do not panic. The ship is under enemy attack. All who have not been assigned battle stations, return to your quarters and await instructions. I repeat, please do not panic."*

Kiril could see plenty of panic, which was all to the good. In the distance she could hear the rumble of explosions. Acting like any panicked passenger, she ran towards the bridge. Three times men running in the opposite direction knocked her down. Each time she picked herself up and ran on, trying not to think of who was on the bridge.

She found the bridge door wide open, with not even a security guard defending it. Probably running for the lifeboats like everybody else, she thought. So much for Satsuma's hiring standards. She darted inside and ducked behind a console. Here there was excitement, but people were staying at their instruments. Veteran officers were calmly giving orders and restoring confidence. Then she saw Izquierda.

The towering form was unmistakable. He stood on an upper terrace, yelling at someone whose image was projected in a full-length screen. Around him stood several officers, including Tomas Huerta. Kiril began to make her way towards him, keeping her eyes peeled for an unoccupied communication set. Everything seemed to be manned. Then she saw who it was Izquierda was yelling at over the set: Admiral Nagamitsu. This was too good to miss.

"Admiral!" Izquierda shouted. "This ship is under enemy attack! I demand that you render assistance!"

"We are on our way, Director," Nagamitsu said, "but I do not see how you can be under attack. Whatever holed your hull is gone and the breach is sealed. Are you trying to tell me that an assault force has boarded your ship?"

"That is exactly what I am saying! There must be hundreds of them, but we can't get a visual fix. They are taking out sensors as they go, cutting power and fuel lines, everything. They are destroying my ship!"

"Director," called an officer. "They've dropped all three mall levels to the keel. Construction personnel at upper-keel level report two Vivers inflicting damage, that is all."

Izquierda turned on the man, all pretense of humanity dropped. "There are no Vivers aboard, you fool!" He smashed the man to the deck with his fist. Kiril could hear the sickening sound of the jaw breaking. "The Vivers are dead! We killed them when we destroyed the *Space Angel*!"

The moment of distraction was all Kiril needed. She darted before the screen, tore the box loose from her belt and hit the pressure plate. "There sure as hell are Vivers aboard this ship! I'm Kiril, from *Space Angel*. I've just sent you coordinates to find her on the planet. Take a look and get here quick, Admiral, this man wants to start a wa—" Iron fingers wrapped around her neck and slammed her into an instrument panel. When she was hauled to her feet, her face was an inch from Izquierda's.

"You!" he said, his rage turning to wonder. "How did you get here?"

"My friends and I came in a Dzuna ship," she managed to choke out. He lightened his grasp a little. "If you want to live and keep your ship, you better do some fast talking."

"Two Vivers?" he said. "Just two Vivers doing all this?"

"Well, I helped a little, but you better not harm me if you don't want to answer to them."

"What do you mean, answer to them?" The unreality of it all had put him into some kind of shock.

"I mean now they're just having fun, you maniac! Hurt me and you'll make them mad!"

He shoved her into Huerta's arms. "Take her to the secure rooms, Tomas. I'll join you later." He turned back to the screen and his mask was back in place.

"What is going on over there, Director?" Nagamitsu demanded.

"Just a distraught clerk, Admiral," Izquierda said. "I've had her taken to the infirmary."

"We'll be aboard in a few minutes, Director." That was the last Kiril heard as Huerta dragged her from the bridge. In all the confusion, had Nagamitsu even heard her?

Huerta hauled her out of the control area, and she could see the people at the consoles looking at her then at each other and jabbering questions. Whatever confidence Izquierda and his officers had restored was fast eroding. Huerta hit a panel and a portal opened. Then they were in a small lift.

In the lift Huerta did not relax his hold, but Kiril could still reach her knives. She decided not to try. Taking Huerta would be easy, but it probably wouldn't do her any good. She could see that this lift had some kind of secure control that she couldn't operate. The lift stopped and the door slid open.

Huerta pulled her down a short hallway and worked the combination of a massive door. It swung open silently and they were inside a room full of instruments and racks of tools and weapons. She recognized a refrigeration unit and a fully equipped medical station. This was some kind of emergency retreat, in case the ship was damaged. Just big enough for a few picked officers, of course. Others didn't rate this kind of care.

Huerta pushed her into an adjacent room, where something hit the back of her knees and she sat heavily. Luckily, it was a low, padded settee. This room was rather bare, but she saw a small airlock hatch in one wall and the universal symbol meaning lifeboat.

Huerta was holding a small pistol on her. "Sure you feel safe?" she taunted. "I'm real dangerous, you know."

"That's true," he said. "The way bacteria are dangerous. I find it hard to believe that my uncle really considered you as a potential member of the family. You're nothing but gutter trash."

So the old monster had really meant it. "That's because your uncle has a lot more brains than you, Tomas. You'd better do some fast thinking if you don't want to end up in the gutter right alongside me."

"What do you mean?" he said. He tried to sound arrogant, but she could hear the weak uncertainty in his voice.

"You got any idea what's happening? It's not an enemy raid, just my two shipmates the Vivers. They'll be coming for me about now. Your uncle's finished, Huerta. His plot's blown wide open and he's facing execution. You better figure a way to escape the same fate."

"Nonsense," Huerta blustered. "The Izquierda wealth and power are immune to laws and courts. My uncle owns governments the way his line owns ships."

"That's what he's been telling you?" She leaned back on the settee, spreading her arms along the backrest. She had this little snake's measure now. "Maybe that's true back in human-controlled space. I hear the powers back there are old and corrupt and his kind helped make it that way. Here it's different.

"On this ship, and coming in this direction, are two Vivers who don't know what wealth is, and their idea of power is the beamers they've got in their hands. Down below is a planetful of warlike people called the Dzuna who never heard of Satsuma but who know, because we proved it to them, that your uncle, and he alone, staged the attack on them. They're fond of revenge. Coming along quick, and maybe here already, is Admiral Nagamitsu. Izquierda may have bought some of the navy people, but Nagamitsu has something against him that goes way back. This ship is sinking, Huerta, it's time to scramble off.'' She watched his expression crumble, as if all the stuffing was running out of him. ''But,'' she went on brightly, ''you just may be the luckiest man aboard this wreck.''

''What do you mean?'' he hissed. The pistol wavered and dropped to his side.

''If you move fast enough, you just might cut a deal with Nagamitsu. He's gonna be real anxious to know who the traitors are aboard his ship. I got a feeling you have that information, right?'' Huerta nodded reluctantly. ''Well, if you run along right now and start selling out as fast as you can, you just might make it before some other turncoat does.''

Huerta stood for a moment, indecisive. Then he thrust the pistol into his belt, turned and ran out, slamming the hatch behind him. Kiril slumped back against the settee, her heart pounding. She'd done it! Well, part of it, anyway. She darted to the hatch and tried it. It was sealed. That wasn't good. All the weapons were in the antechamber. She tried the access to the lifeboat, but she didn't know how to open it. It was probably keyed for ship's officers anyway.

She returned to the settee. If she could make the next few minutes in one piece, she might just get out of this alive. It was a hope she'd already abandoned, and its return was painful. She turned her head towards the hatch as a hiss of hydraulic fluid reached her ear. It swung slowly open. Framed in the hatchway was Izquierda. So much for hope.

He stepped in. ''Where is Tomas?'' He might have been talking about the weather. He crossed to the lifeboat hatch and began working its combination.

''He's running to blab everything to Nagamitsu while it's worth something. Did you think he'd stick with you? He's dumb, but he's not *that* dumb.''

He turned on her with that heart-freezing glare, the reptile within fully exposed at last. For some reason, it didn't paralyze her this time. "It's *her* doing, isn't it? Your Captain Gertrude HaLevy. She hounded me out of the navy in the War, now she's trying to destroy me. I want those coordinates. She's down there someplace and I am going to kill her."

"Has anybody ever told you how crazy you are?" Kiril asked.

"What is it you want?" He seemed to be sincerely puzzled. "A Satsuma directorship? It's yours, the one Tomas would have had. Wealth and power beyond your ability to imagine."

"You just don't get it, do you?" she said.

"Then how about this?" He drew a small hand beamer and aimed it at her. Kiril seemed to huddle in upon herself, drawing in her arms and legs, but her hands were on her dagger hilts and her legs were coiled under her. It wasn't in her to give up. Maybe, even with a beamer hole burned through her, she could still get him. "You can keep your life if you give me those coordinates."

"You can't buy it all, Ramon," she said, preparing to spring.

"She's quite right, you know." Izquierda whirled towards the hatch, but something lashed into his hand and the pistol went spinning across the chamber. Standing in the hatch she saw the bulky figure of Nagamitsu. Behind him were K'Stin and B'Shant. The admiral stepped in with K'Stin behind him.

"You are well, skinny one?" K'Stin asked.

"Fine," she said. The Viver nodded curtly.

"We can deal, Admiral," Izquierda said.

"No, we can't," said Nagamitsu. "Your nephew had an interesting tale to tell. I've already ordered a good number of my people clapped in irons. I don't like doing that, but it's a better ship now. On the way up here my friend K'Stin has been giving me a brief account of what has been happening down on that planet. I've seen the real *Space Angel*. She is intact."

"You are not going to take that woman's account seriously, Admiral?"

"Her account is quite irrelevant. The ship which you claimed to have destroyed is in one piece. I had thought your story farfetched to begin with, and this is the clinching argument. For whatever insane reasons of your own, you have tried to maneuver us into a war with this extremely powerful people and blame it all on one lonely little tramp freighter."

"It was a business matter," Izquierda said with a shrug.

"Ah, yes, business. That is your justification for everything. You should have stuck to corrupt, greedy men like yourself, Director. You should not have tried to involve these people. Most particularly you should not have tried to use young Kiril here. She seems quite resourceful."

Izquierda glared at her. "So she is. Am I to regard myself as under arrest, Admiral? You know it won't do any good. I can control any court I come before."

"Possibly so, but it won't come to that."

"What do you mean?"

Nagamitsu touched the long handle of the sword in his belt. "Because, technically, we are at war. That was your doing, Director. As supreme commander in this sector I have the right of summary execution."

"You don't dare," Izquierda said.

"You are wrong. I confess, Director, that for many years I have despaired of ever reaching you. Your layers of protection separated us, and a retired admiral has little influence in peacetime. And now here we are, just the two of us."

"I don't understand," Izquierda said.

"It was the incident on Delta Orion Five, Director," Nagamitsu said without emotion. "You sent half your force to deal with the Triumvirate ships while you got your ships and cargoes away. Do you remember who was in charge of that squadron?"

Izquierda shook his head. "I confess, I do not."

"I suppose you wouldn't. You had weighty matters of business to concern you. It was Under-Commodore Masaharu Katsu. He was my eldest daughter's husband. She was serving aboard a hospital ship at the time. When she received the news, she cycled herself through an airlock without a pressure suit. It was a demonstration of grief, a protest against the injustice of her husband's death and a reminder to her father that this thing must not go unavenged."

Izquierda smiled thinly. "So that's it. It's really a personal matter, isn't it? You are going to have your revenge on me and use your wartime powers to hide it."

"No," Nagamitsu said, "I will not execute you over a personal matter, but I will challenge you. This stain upon my family honor must be wiped out. The spirits of my daughter and my son-in-law must be given rest." He signaled, and K'Stin dropped a long sword at Izquierda's feet. "Wait outside," he told the Vivers.

Izquierda bent and picked up the sword. "I can't say much for your judgment, Admiral," he said. "You should never give a man a bare blade while your own is sheathed." He lunged. Kiril had never seen anything as fast as Nagamitsu's move in unsheathing his sword. She closed her eyes tightly for a second. When she opened them, the admiral was calmly cleaning his blade.

"This sword has been in my family for seven hundred years," he said. "This is foul blood to stain so noble a blade." When it was clean, he sheathed it in one smooth, graceful motion, without looking at the scabbard. He took her hand. "Come along, my dear. Let's go see what we can do about your ship."

Wearily, she let him lead her back outside.

13

Kiril studied Earth through the observation bubble. They were in a low orbit and the view was spectacular. She'd had a chance to go down to the home planet with a landing party, but she had backed out. The others had told her that Earth was no longer beautiful from close up, and in any case she had already half decided never to set foot off *Space Angel* again.

"*Kiril*," Nancy called, "come on down. Skipper's called a meeting." Most of the ship's personnel had been on the nearby dock station for a couple of days. They had been under orders to say nothing of what had occurred on and near the Dzuna planet until they received permission. She went through the navigator's room and down the corridor to the mess room.

"Everyone here?" the skipper asked. "Okay, here's the word we got: First of all, nothing, I repeat, absolutely *nothing* happened back there except routine diplomatic negotiations. Apparently they got the Dzuna to agree to keep quiet, too. After all, nothing much happened to them. All records of the events on and near the planet have been put under hundred-year seal.

Any one of us or anybody else who was along on the expedition that talks out of line is guilty of treason.''

Everybody began to talk at once. "It figures!" Torwald said. "They aren't going to let a little matter like this embarrass them.''

"That's right," the skipper said. "The events out there uncovered widespread corruption in the government and the military. There's a housecleaning going on right now, orchestrated mainly by Nagamitsu and Pierce, but that's going to be kept quiet as well. Mustn't alarm the voters, you know.''

"But surely they're going to break up Satsuma!" Michelle protested.

"Why?" asked the skipper. "Nothing happened, remember? In fact, I hear the government's going to pay for the repair of the damages their Supernova sustained in the regrettable accident in which Director Izquierda was so regrettably killed.''

"All that good work gone to waste!" K'Stin said bitterly.

Bert turned to Kiril with a tired smile. "You see, Kiril, how wisely you chose in staying with a free freighter working at the fringes of human space?" She nodded.

"On the plus side, they've finally released our funds from the impounded diamond crystal cargo, with accumulated interest.'' There was prolonged cheering.

"We're rich!" Finn said.

"Not exactly," the skipper said. The cheering died down. "I've already sent Kelly his share, he's still aboard Probert's *Black Comet*." She turned to Kiril. "Kelly was the ship's boy on that trip." Kiril nodded. She'd heard all about it, over and over.

"The upshot is this: You all know the customs of free freighters. The truth is the *Space Angel*'s a wreck. She needs a new thruster. She has to undergo a complete hull rebuilding to seal all the cracks and leaks. Half our instruments have to be replaced and all the internal bulkheads have been weakened. It means weeks in airdock even after we scrounge all the parts. Just finding that class of thruster and buying it will cost a fortune.

"Anybody who wants to leave the ship can collect his share and go. If you decide to stay, your share goes into the common fund to keep the ship alive. Once we're spaceworthy again, we'll have to refuel and reprovision. With luck we might just break even.''

"She has to have the work," Torwald agreed. "If the Dzuna hadn't lifted us from that swamp and we hadn't come back in the hold of the TFCS, we never would've made it back at all. My share stays with the *Angel*."

"Anybody choose to leave?" She looked around. Nobody wanted to go. "That's it, then. Come on, people, we've got work to do."

Later Kiril found the skipper alone on the bridge. "Come on in," the skipper said. "You been giving it some thought?"

"Yes," Kiril said. "I've been talking with Bert. He's got to retire before long, and he wants me to apprentice with him. It sounds good to me."

The skipper nodded. "It's a good position. But keep in mind what I said about going to school to be a bridge officer. You're good material, kid. Don't let it go to waste."

"I'll think about it," she said. "But things have been coming at me too fast. I want to take it slow for a while."

The skipper grinned around her cigar. "That's smart, Kiril. You've got plenty of time. Maybe we all have." She slapped a bulkhead and it resounded solidly. "This old girl's got a lot of years left in her." She turned back to Kiril. "We've got about a ton of second-hand instruments coming in within the hour, and getting them in and stored is the cargo master's job. Get to work!"

Kiril dashed down the companionway and through the corridor toward the hold. Already she was planning where she would store the instruments.

MORE SCIENCE FICTION ADVENTURE!

☐ 0-441-38291-6	**JANISSARIES**, Jerry E. Pournelle	$3.50
☐ 0-441-78042-3	**STAR COLONY**, Keith Laumer	$3.95
☐ 0-441-31602-6	**HAMMER'S SLAMMERS**, David Drake	$2.95
☐ 0-441-09019-2	**CADRE LUCIFER**, Robert O'Riordan	$2.95
☐ 0-425-09776-5	**CIRCUIT BREAKER**, Melinda M. Snodgrass	$2.95
☐ 0-425-09560-6	**DOME**, Michael Reaves and Steve Perry	$3.50
☐ 0-441-10602-1	**CITIZEN PHAID**, Mick Farren	$2.95
☐ 0-441-77913-1	**THE STAINLESS STEEL RAT SAVES THE WORLD**, Harry Harrison	$2.95
☐ 0-441-08934-8	**BURNING CHROME**, William Gibson	$2.95
☐ 0-441-85456-7	**THE UNIVERSE BETWEEN**, Alan E. Nourse	$2.95

Please send the titles I've checked above. Mail orders to:

BERKLEY PUBLISHING GROUP
390 Murray Hill Pkwy., Dept. B
East Rutherford. NJ 07073

NAME _____

ADDRESS _____

CITY _____

STATE _____ ZIP _____

Please allow 6 weeks for delivery.
Prices are subject to change without notice.

POSTAGE & HANDLING:
$1.00 for one book, $.25 for each
additional. Do not exceed $3.50.

BOOK TOTAL	$_____
SHIPPING & HANDLING	$_____
APPLICABLE SALES TAX (CA, NJ, NY, PA)	$_____
TOTAL AMOUNT DUE PAYABLE IN US FUNDS. (No cash orders accepted.)	$_____

ACE
SCIENCE FICTION
SPECIALS

Under the brilliant editorship of Terry Carr,
the award-winning <u>Ace Science Fiction Specials</u>
were <u>the</u> imprint for literate, quality sf.

Now, once again under the leadership of Terry Carr,
<u>The New Ace SF Specials</u> have been created
to seek out the talents and titles that will lead
science fiction into the 21st Century.

— THE WILD SHORE   0-441-88874-7/$3.50
    Kim Stanley Robinson
— NEUROMANCER   0-441-56959-5/$2.95
    William Gibson
— IN THE DRIFT   0-441-35869-1/$2.95
    Michael Swanwick
— THE HERCULES TEXT   0-441-37367-4/$3.50
    Jack McDevitt
— THE NET   0-441-56941-2/$2.95
    Loren J. MacGregor

<u>Please send the titles I've checked above.</u> Mail orders to:

BERKLEY PUBLISHING GROUP
390 Murray Hill Pkwy., Dept. B
East Rutherford, NJ 07073

NAME _____

ADDRESS _____

CITY _____

STATE _____ ZIP _____

Please allow 6 weeks for delivery.
Prices are subject to change without notice.

POSTAGE & HANDLING:
$1.00 for one book, $.25 for each
additional. Do not exceed $3.50.

BOOK TOTAL $_____

SHIPPING & HANDLING $_____

APPLICABLE SALES TAX $_____
(CA, NJ, NY, PA)

TOTAL AMOUNT DUE $_____
PAYABLE IN US FUNDS.
(No cash orders accepted.)

SCIENCE FICTION AT ITS BEST!

____ **THE CAT WHO WALKS THROUGH WALLS**
Robert A. Heinlein   0-425-09932-8 — $3.95

____ **TITAN**
John Varley   0-441-81304-6 — $3.95

____ **DUNE**
Frank Herbert   0-441-17266-0 — $4.50

____ **HERETICS OF DUNE**
Frank Herbert   0-425-08732-8 — $4.50

____ **GODS OF RIVERWORLD**
Philip José Farmer   0-425-09170-8 — $3.50

____ **THE MAN IN THE HIGH CASTLE**
Philip K. Dick   0-425-10143-6 — $2.95

____ **HELLICONIA SUMMER**
Brian W. Aldiss   0-425-08650-X — $3.95

____ **THE GREEN PEARL**
Jack Vance   0-441-30316-1 — $3.95

____ **DOLPHIN ISLAND**
Arthur C. Clarke   0-441-15220-1 — $2.95

Please send the titles I've checked above. Mail orders to:

BERKLEY PUBLISHING GROUP
390 Murray Hill Pkwy., Dept. B
East Rutherford, NJ 07073

NAME _____

ADDRESS _____

CITY _____

STATE _____ ZIP _____

Please allow 6 weeks for delivery.
Prices are subject to change without notice.

POSTAGE & HANDLING:
$1.00 for one book, $.25 for each
additional. Do not exceed $3.50.

BOOK TOTAL $_____

SHIPPING & HANDLING $_____

APPLICABLE SALES TAX $_____
(CA, NJ, NY, PA)

TOTAL AMOUNT DUE $_____
PAYABLE IN US FUNDS.
(No cash orders accepted.)

440

Book Four of the Apprentice Adept Series
by
New York Times Bestselling Author

PIERS ANTHONY

OUT OF PHAZE

*Welcome to the astonishing parallel
worlds of Phaze and Proton. Where magic
and science maintain an uneasy truce. Where an
accidental mind-switch plunges an apprentice
wizard from Phaze into the mind-boggling
technology of Proton. And where a robot named
Mach is, in turn, swept away to a world
of bizarre and terrifying wonders:
the dazzling world of Phaze…*

OUT OF PHAZE   0-441-64465-1/$3.95

Please send the titles I've checked above. Mail orders to:

BERKLEY PUBLISHING GROUP
390 Murray Hill Pkwy., Dept. B
East Rutherford, NJ 07073

NAME _____

ADDRESS _____

CITY _____

STATE _____ ZIP _____

Please allow 6 weeks for delivery.
Prices are subject to change without notice.

POSTAGE & HANDLING:
$1.00 for one book, $.25 for each
additional. Do not exceed $3.50.

BOOK TOTAL	$_____
SHIPPING & HANDLING	$_____
APPLICABLE SALES TAX (CA, NJ, NY, PA)	$_____
TOTAL AMOUNT DUE	$_____

PAYABLE IN US FUNDS.
(No cash orders accepted.)